Cookery

Gardening

Features

Puzzles

Horoscopes

£5.99

Celebrating 100 YEARS of MILLS & BOON

The year 2008 is a special one for all of us here at Mills & Boon because we're celebrating our centenary!

In 1908 Gerald Mills and Charles Boon joined forces to create Mills & Boon Ltd. Although now known the world over for its romances, the company was not founded as a romance fiction publishing house, but our first book, *Arrows from the Dark* by Sophie Cole, was, prophetically, a romance.

> **Fact:** Did you know a Mills & Boon book is sold every two seconds around the world?

Those early years saw Mills & Boon publish a huge range of books from fiction to cooking! We were the first to publish *Phantom of the Opera* by Gaston Leroux in English. We also had a wide variety of authors — including Georgette Heyer, E.F. Benson, Hugh Walpole,

> **Fact:** Did you know three Mills & Boon novels were placed in a time capsule celebrating 60 years of the BBC 'since Mills & Boon books are read by an enormous section of the British public'?

and Maire Van Vorst. P.G. Wodehouse even published a novel, The *Prince and Betty*, with Mills & Boon in May 1912. We also printed a number of books by Jack London, including *The Jacket* and *Hearts of Three*.

From the very beginning, Mills & Boon published in a form and at a price that was within the reach of a wide readership. In the 1930s the romance genre was very popular and the company decided to concentrate on hardback romances, and so the Mills & Boon we know today was born! The books were sold

through weekly two-penny libraries and their distinctive brown bindings led them to become known as 'the books in brown'.

With the decline of lending libraries in the late 1950s, the company's most successful move was to realise that readers wanted easy access to reasonably priced books. As a result Mills & Boon romance became widely available from newsagents across the country.

Over the years, we've published some incredible authors under the Mills & Boon banner. Space permits us to mention just two. Mary Burchell, who began writing for us in the 1930s and continued to do so for another half a century, helped many Jews flee Nazi Germany in the years before the Second World War and continued to be involved in philanthropic causes and refugee relief for the rest of her life. Betty Neels, whose books are international best-sellers, trained as a nurse and midwife. She was an army nursing sister during the war,

eventually marrying a Dutch doctor. But Betty only started to write on her retirement from nursing, motivated by a lady in a library bemoaning the lack of romantic novels.

Mills & Boon's centenary is a chance to celebrate our first 100 years of wonderful romance and fiction—the books, the authors and our readers—and of course look forward to the next 100 years!

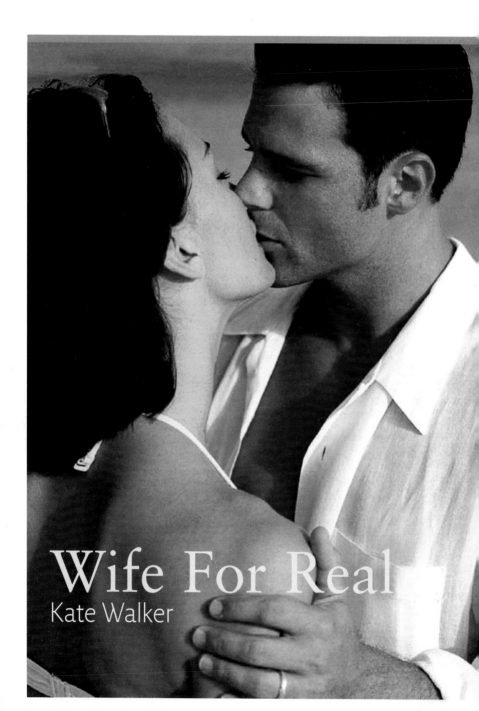

Wife For Real
Kate Walker

'So you're my wife, are you? Well, that's interesting!'

Eyes the colour of a storm-heavy sky raked over Louise's slender figure as she stood in the doorway of her cottage, so transfixed by shock that she was unable to move. Even the jeans and warm cherry-red sweater she wore were suddenly no protection against the cold.

'Tell me, *mi esposa*...' He laced the words with dark satire. 'When exactly were you going to inform me of this fact?'

'I wasn't...'

It was all that Louise could manage. In the moments since she had opened the front door in response to an imperious and impatient sounding knock, she barely recognised her world in the centre of the emotional tornado that whirled around her.

But she certainly recognised the man who stood on her doorstep. Eight years was a long time, but she would know Alex anywhere. His sort of superb bone structure only got better with age. He was too tall, too dark, too imposing — too devastating physically — ever to forget, even if she didn't have deeply personal reasons for never being able to put him out of her mind.

'You weren't?'

The darkly satirical tone deepened on the question.

'You weren't going to tell me — your *husband* — of this secret marriage? Didn't you think that would be wise, or at least courteous, *querida*?'

'No.'

It was the honest truth. She had certainly never thought that her foolish and impulsive declaration would ever have been believed by anyone. And she had definitely *never* thought that it would reach the ears of Alex Anderson — Alex Alcolar, as she supposed she must now think of him since he had taken his father's name. He was hundreds of miles away, living his new life in Spain. He would never hear of her, or spare her a thought, let alone give a damn about the unthinking cover-up she had used in a moment of crisis.

But it seemed that he had. And what had been purely and simply an impulsive act of defence had turned into another unneeded complication in her life.

The worst sort of complication of all. She did *not* want Alex back in her life.

'I wasn't going to tell you any of it. So who did?'

Alex shrugged broad shoulders under a fine leather jacket.

'I don't know. I received an anonymous letter, posted in this village, telling me that I was neglecting my wife. The wife I didn't know I had. So naturally I came as quickly as I could.'

'But you must have known that the "marriage" wasn't a real one. And that it had nothing to do with you.'

'Nothing?' His echoing of the word was riddled with scepticism and mockery. 'If you're using my name, claiming to be my wife, then I think it has everything to do with me. As I recall, when you knew me before, your father didn't think I was fit to associate with your family, and you ended up swallowing everything he said. Now suddenly you're claiming to be married to me! So I think you'd better start explaining. Start by telling me where, exactly, this wedding took place.'

'You don't really need me to answer that, do you?' Louise tossed at him, hazel eyes sparking defiance. 'Because you know where — *exactly*. Nowhere! The wedding didn't take place anywhere. As you are only too aware, there was no wedding ever!'

To her surprise he actually smiled, the curve of his lips and the light in his clear grey eyes brightening his whole face and making her stomach turn over, her pulse quicken in instant response.

'I'm glad to hear that. I was beginning to wonder if my mind was going. Or at least my memory — because I have no recollection...'

'Of course you don't! And there's nothing wrong with your mind, as you know only too well. You've not forgotten anything. In fact, you must have known that all this was nonsense in the first place — so why, exactly, are you here now? What on earth made you travel all the way from — from... ?'

'From Andalusia,' Alex supplied. 'That's where I live now.'

'Of course. That's why you're suddenly littering your conversation with Spanish phrases!'

The Alex she had once known hadn't spoken a word of Spanish. He hadn't even known that he had any Spanish connections — that the blood of a Spanish aristocrat ran in his veins. It had only been after his mother had died that he had discovered the truth about his father.

'I am Spanish,' Alex put in coldly. 'At least, half-Spanish. My father is Spanish. My home and my work are in Andalusia. Most days I speak nothing but Spanish.'

'Which makes it all the more puzzling why you've bothered to come here...'

And that was a question that he had been asking himself for days, Alex admitted.

Why was he travelling to England on what was little more than a whim?

Why had he snatched at the smallest excuse to get on a plane and head straight back to the village where he had grown up? The village that he believed he had left far behind in his past, where it belonged. He thought he'd shaken the dust of the place from his feet and that he would never, ever go back to the woman who had once almost destroyed his life — and yet now here he was.

So why?

Because he hadn't been able to help himself.

'I wanted to meet the woman who claimed to be my wife.'

His beautiful mouth curved into a smile that made Louise's blood run cold.

'I wanted to see what had become of you.'

'Nothing exciting, as you can see. In fact nothing at all!'

The rather wild hand gesture took in herself and her surroundings, betraying more than she wanted to reveal. These were not at all the conditions in which she had lived in the past. And she knew from the way that Alex's eyes narrowed swiftly that he, too, was remembering how it had once been.

'What happened?'

It was cold, crisp, incisive. She didn't want to answer, but she knew he wouldn't let her dodge the question.

'Do you mean why am I here, in this cottage, instead of up at the manor house where I used to be? Things change, Alex! Nothing remains the same.'

'You have,' he put in sharply. 'You haven't changed. You're still as beautiful as ever.'

It was the last thing she had expected, and it hit her with the force of a blow to her chest, driving all the breath from her body. And what made matters worse was the new and disturbing darkness that hadn't been there before in those grey eyes. A darkness that spoke of physical arousal and a smouldering sensuality that stirred memories she had thought long buried.

Memories she wanted to stay hidden.

'No...' she managed huskily, not at all sure precisely what she was saying no to.

'Yes,' Alex countered, the single word rough on his tongue. 'You're just as lovely as you always were. More, if that were possible...'

The single step he took forward broke the spell that seemed to have coiled around her. It brought him too close. Too near. Another couple of movements and he would have been right here in her house — her *home* — and that would be more than she could bear.

'No!' she cried, much more emphatically this time.

Whirling, she dashed into the cottage, slamming the door right in his face.

'Go away!' she shouted, praying her words would reach him through the thickness of the wooden barrier. 'I don't want you here!'

The silence was unexpected and disturbing. Could he really have gone? Could it have been that easy?

It wasn't.

She barely had time to even think about relaxing when a faint sound from the back of the house had her stiffening again.

The dash through to the kitchen must have only taken seconds, but she was still too late. The back door opened and Alex stepped into the tiny room, kicking the door shut and leaning back against it.

'All right, Louise,' he said. 'Don't you think it's about time you started explaining?'

CHAPTER TWO

'Well?' Alex demanded when the seconds

that had ticked away since he had asked the question grew into minutes and still Louise hadn't answered him. 'Are you going to tell me just what's going on?'

'Nothing. Nothing that would interest you anyway.'

'Ah, but there you're wrong. I *am* interested. And you have to admit that I have cause. After all, why would you suddenly claim to be my wife when we haven't seen each other for over eight years? When all that there ever was between us was an adolescent fling that was over before it started?'

Liar! his conscience reproved him. It might have been an adolescent fling to her, but to him it had been the forming relationship of his life. The relationship against which he had measured every woman he had ever met since — and found them lacking. And if he wanted the reason why he was here, back where he had sworn he would never be again, then it was quite painfully simple.

It could be summed up in two short words.

Louise Browning.

He had never forgotten her. Never been able to get her out of his mind.

And given half an excuse to come back and see her again, he had been on the plane before he had even had time for second thoughts.

'So what I want to know is just why you should lay claim to the name of a man you hated, a man who...'

'I never hated you!' Louise broke in sharply, unable to let that go.

'No?'

'No!'

And it wasn't just 'an adolescent fling', she wanted to add. She had adored him. Loved him with all the strength of her young heart. And he had broken that heart when he had walked out of her life for good, leaving her alone and pregnant.

Oh no—no! She could not — must not — think of Gabrielle. To do so would destroy her. Especially now, with the living example of her daughter's heritage standing right there in front of her. If her baby had lived would she have had Alex's dark colouring, those beautiful grey eyes...?

Desperately she forced her attention back to the present.

'Well, you certainly gave me the impression that you couldn't stand the sight of me,' Alex drawled. 'That you wanted me out of your life for good.'

'As I recall, *you* were the one claiming that it was over and done with.'

She had come to him to tell him that she was carrying his child, and he had refused to listen.

'You were on your way out to your new life — your new family in Spain.'

'Louise, I had nothing to keep me here. My mother was dead.'

You didn't want me...

'My father had suddenly decided to acknowledge my existence. I was barely twenty-one and a whole new future suddenly offered itself. I had lost my job, narrowly avoided ending up in prison...'

Alex pushed himself away from the door and came to stand in the middle of the room, his hands on his hips. Looking at them, Louise felt shivers of sensual awareness slide down her spine. It was impossible not to recall the pleasure those hands had given her in the past.

'Tell me, did you really think that I was callous enough to have left you asleep after making love to you and gone though your parents' house, helping myself — '

'I didn't know what to think. I woke up and I was alone.'

'So would you have preferred that I stayed? And been found there when your father came home? That *would* have been fun.'

'But then I found that all my stepmother's jewellery had gone...'

And foolishly she'd swallowed her father's belief that Alex wasn't to be trusted.

'So you told your parents everything. You must have known they'd hit the roof.'

'I couldn't just keep quiet.'

'No, you did the one thing guaranteed to raise your father's blood pressure even higher. You let him know that I had taken his precious daughter's virginity. Tell me, Louise...' Alex levered himself away from the table and began to prowl round the small kitchen '...did you really think that would help me get a fair hearing?'

'I didn't know what else to say,' Louise admitted edgily.

She wished he would stand still — or sit down — anything other than this disturbingly restless movement. He seemed too big, too powerful, too elemental to be enclosed in the confined space of the tiny room. And her own guilt and the bitterness of her memories blended uneasily with the potently sexual appeal he seemed to project without any effort to produce a dangerously explosive combination.

'I felt hurt — more than hurt. I felt betrayed! I thought you'd used me. I was only nineteen. If it makes you feel any better, when I found out that Geoff Thornton had been caught trying to sell the jewellery, I hated myself. I never thought they'd sack you anyway.'

'No?'

Alex had come to stand in front of her, looking down into her pale face surrounded by the tumble of soft brown hair. Those changeable eyes were deep mossy green in this light, clouded with anxiety.

'What did you think they'd do? Welcome the gardener — the housekeeper's son — into the family? The Brownings of Helpcote Manor? You were young, Louise, but not that foolish.'

Moving this close to her had been a mistake, Alex admitted to himself. A big mistake. When he'd kept his distance he'd also been able to keep control of his feelings. But up close like this he could see the peach-fine texture of her skin, smell the faint floral scent of some soap or body lotion she had used.

They said that scent was the sense most likely to evoke powerful memories, and right now he could well believe it was true. Sensual hunger clawed at him instantly and cruelly and the burn of it roughened his voice when he spoke, though this time on a very different note.

'We were both young then. But we've grown up since. I know I have, and you...'

He reached out and closed both hands over the delicate bones of her shoulders.

'You've changed from a lovely girl into a beautiful, desirable woman...'

Not this.

The words sounded in Louise's head but she couldn't force them out on to her tongue. Her throat seemed to have seized up, her lips frozen, and all she could do was wait for the kiss that she knew was coming. The kiss that she could read he wanted in the darkness of his eyes.

> **Fact:** 25th December was not celebrated as the birthday of Christ until the year AD 440.

It was his gentleness that shocked her. The almost delicate, slow taking of her mouth brushed away her doubts, her fears, her hesitation on a sigh of sheer delight. She felt her senses swim, her heart kick up a beat.

The last time he had kissed her they had both been so young, not much more than adolescents. He had kissed her like a boy, with a boy's urgency and impatient hunger. Now he kissed her like a man — a man who knew exactly how to treat a woman. He made her feel intensely female, totally sensual, all woman.

And she wanted more.

With another sigh, a very different one this time, she moved closer, slid her hands up around his neck, pulling his head down towards hers to deepen the kiss. She let her tongue dance with his, heard the heavy thud of his heart, felt the heated pressure of his desire against the softness of her stomach, and the *no* that had formed in her thoughts melted away into a deep and totally submissive *yes, oh, yes*!

'No!'

It was Alex who spoke this time. And his tone made it plain that there was no room for argument, no chance of debate.

His body spoke more clearly than his words, stiffening and pulling away from her, twisting free of her clinging hands and leaving her feeling cold and lost and desperately alone.

'No!' he said, more forcefully this time. 'This is not going to happen.'

The fight he was having against the demands of his senses made it sound far harsher, more brutal than he had actually intended, but perhaps that was just as well. In the past he had let his physical responses to Louise drown out the warning cries of his thoughts — and look where that had got him.

Homeless, unemployed and facing

possible criminal charges.

Well, he'd learned his lesson. Things had to be very different this time.

'This is not what I came here for.'

'Oh, isn't it?' The misery of rejection forced the words from her. 'I thought it was exactly what you wanted!'

'Well, then, you thought wrong. The only thing I want is an explanation. I want to know why you're using my name when you have no right to.'

CHAPTER THREE

'You want an explanation! You want to know why I'm using your name! A name I have "no right to"! You've got very arrogant since you exchanged Alcolar for Anderson!'

'If you mean I don't bow and scrape to the lady of the manor any more,' Alex tossed back, 'I don't do that for anyone. So are you going to explain why you're suddenly claiming to be my wife?'

'I told you...'

Alex's wide, sensual mouth twisted cynically as his grey eyes flicked over her dismissively.

'You told me "nothing's going on".'

Then, just as Louise nerved herself for more, he suddenly shocked her totally by switching on a smile. But it was a smile that was totally lacking in warmth; his eyes were shards of ice.

'Ok,' he said. 'If that's the way you want it...'

And to Louise's horror he turned and headed straight for the door.

Would she let him go? he wondered. Or would she weaken and call him back? He had seen the shadows in her eyes and wondered privately just what had put them there.

Another step or two and his fingers had closed over the door handle. Turned it.

Behind him he heard Louise draw in a deep, raw-edged sigh and let it out again in a despondent rush.

'Alex. Please...I — I need your help.'

* * *

'Where exactly are we going?'

Alex's patience was rapidly wearing thin. When Louise had admitted that she needed his help, he had thought that at last they were getting somewhere. But she hadn't explained a thing. Instead, she had snatched a coat from the hook in the hall, told him to come with her and headed out into the biting wind and threatening rain of a January afternoon.

'You'll see when we get there.'

All right, let her be mysterious. He didn't have to stick around if it didn't suit him.

But this journey was bringing back memories. Memories that told him they were heading for the manor house.

He'd walked this way often enough in his youth. The journey from the village had been one he had made almost every day when he'd worked in the gardens there and his mother had been the housekeeper.

But, of course, he'd made the journey with Louise at his side. Their brief, passionate relationship had had to be conducted in secret, for fear that her parents might find out.

'Is this car really yours?'

Louise knew she was only speaking to fill the awkward silence. She was sharply, disturbingly aware of Alex's size and strength beside her in the confined space. The rangy youth she had known had grown into a powerful and intensely masculine man. The wild wind outside had tossed his black hair over his forehead and tiny diamonds of raindrops sparkled in the jet-dark strands.

'Well, I certainly didn't steal it if that's what you're thinking.'

'I never thought any such thing!'

But her conscience told her that she had only herself to blame for the cynical dig.

'I should have trusted you,' she blurted out before her courage deserted her.

'What?'

Louise snatched in a sharp, calming breath, trying to suppress the million butterflies that had suddenly started beating frantic wings deep inside her stomach.

'I should have known that you wouldn't have stolen my stepmother's jewellery.'

She should have listened to her heart instead of her head.

But wasn't the truth that her weak, foolish heart had been totally untrustworthy, too? Her heart had told her that in Alex she had found the love of her life, the man with whom she wanted to spend all her

tomorrows. But he had had what he'd wanted from her and then he'd turned his back on her.

She should have realised what had been coming that morning — the morning after he'd taken her virginity — when she'd woken up and found herself alone. What was it he had said when she'd gone to him to try to tell him about the baby?

'It was fun, darling, but not that special.' And then he'd left. He'd gone to live his new life in Spain, and he hadn't spared her a single thought.

'Melissa was spitting nails, as I remember.'

Alex's casual tone belied the tautness of his jaw, the way that every hard line of his profile was pulled tight over his stunning bone structure. Louise's lack of faith in him had been a betrayal that had savaged his soul.

'I think she was truly disappointed to discover that it was Thornton who actually had all her diamonds.'

He steered the car carefully around an awkward bend.

'So where is she now?'

Louise shifted awkwardly on the soft leather seat, the movement bringing a wave of soft, floral scent that stirred his senses cruelly. His hands tightened on the steering wheel.

'In Australia. She married again soon after my father died.'

'Yes, I heard about that. I'm sorry.'

'It was very sudden. A heart attack.'

'That must have been hard on you.'

Louise managed a mumble that might have been agreement. Her father's death had been a terrible shock, but she hadn't been prepared for the problems that had followed after it. She hadn't really had time to mourn him before her world had collapsed around her.

'Turn here,' she said, as much to distract herself as to direct him.

'I gathered this was — What the hell...?'

Alex slammed on the brakes with nothing like his usual care or skill. As soon as the car had come to a halt he was out of the car and standing, staring around him in disbelief and confusion.

The big old house that had once been so loved and cared for now stood empty and neglected. The ivy that climbed up one wall was overgrown and wild, as were the lawns that edged the gravelled driveway. Weeds poked up from every flowerbed, and the rose garden that had once been Louise's father's pride and joy was just a tangle of withered blooms and unpruned branches.

But what shocked him most of all was the large, roughly painted sign: *Private property. Keep out! Trespassers will be prosecuted*.

'What happened here?'

Louise got out of the car and came to stand beside him, looking very vulnerable and lost as she huddled into her coat.

'Geoff Thornton happened,' she said miserably. 'When he got out of prison he came back here.'

'And?' Alex prompted harshly, because there had to be an *and*.

'And he managed to make some money — legal or not, I don't know. He set himself up in a casino.'

Her hazel eyes, sheening with unshed tears, slid to the desolation of the old house, and Alex thought he understood.

'And your father — '

'No!' she interrupted him, shaking her head emphatically so that her soft brown hair flew around her pale face. 'Not my father — Melissa. My stepmother got hooked on gambling. She lost — heavily. My father found out and paid her debts once and she promised it wouldn't happen again.'

'But it did?'

'Yes.' It was low and miserable. 'It happened again. Much worse this time. She lost a fortune, and Geoff Thornton wanted his money. I think it was the shock of the demand that brought on the heart attack that killed my father. She'd lost everything. There was no way we could repay him except...'

'Except by letting him have the manor?'

'Yes. And he didn't even want it to live in. He just let it go to rack and ruin. I think he just wanted to have his revenge on us for putting him in prison that time.'

But Alex wasn't listening. He was fighting the red haze of fury that was raging inside, destroying his ability to think.

The house that had been in the Browning

family for centuries. Louise had always loved the manor. She had once said that she would do anything to keep it.

Anything.

Including claiming to be married to him?

She hadn't thought him worthy to be with her before. But now that he was rich and could afford a house like this...

He felt sick — furious — used.

'This help you need, *querida*...does it involve saving the ancestral family home?'

It involved much more than that. She had had such dreams for the manor.... But she didn't dare to tell him the rest.

'Yes, it does,' she said hesitantly.

'And what do I get in return?'

Louise swallowed hard, forcing herself to meet the darkness in his eyes.

'Anything,' she croaked. 'Just ask. If I can manage it, I'll do it. What did you have in mind?'

Alex's smile was cold as the sleet-laden wind that swirled around them.

'Oh, I'm sure that I'll think of something.'

CHAPTER FOUR

Alex drew his car to a halt outside the cottage and sat for a moment, scowling through the windshield at the other vehicle already parked outside Louise's cottage.

Someone had got here before him, and he wasn't in the mood for polite conversation. There were questions he wanted answers to — and fast. And they weren't the sort of questions he wanted to discuss in front of anyone else.

For a moment or two he considered turning around and driving away again, but then he changed his mind. He wanted this business over and done with as soon as possible.

Done with?

Face it, he told himself as he got out of the car and slammed the door behind him. Nothing about Louise had ever been 'done with'.

He might have thought that he had been 'over' her when he had left the village and gone to live in Spain, but he had been deluding himself to believe so. And coming back here had just proved it.

In five minutes flat she had got under his skin as strongly as ever, and he had been forced to admit that nothing had died. Seeing her had simply revived all the hunger that he had felt when he had known her before. Revived it so strongly that he'd spent his nights enduring wild, erotic dreams about her, waking up hard and aching. And when he was with her he felt as if he had lost all the years in between, being once more reduced to the yearning, lustful state of the nineteen-year-old he had been when he had first met her.

That was why he was here now.

He had told himself that now that he knew exactly what Louise wanted from him, he would pack his bags and get out of there — fast. All she saw him as was a wealthy man who could restore her precious manor — and along with it the status of the Browning family — to its former glory. So was he going to let himself be used like that?

No way!

At least that was what he had told himself three days ago. He was getting on the next plane back to Spain and...

And here he was at Louise's front door again.

He had cursed his stupidity, told himself he was every sort of a fool. But he hadn't been able to get Louise out of his mind in eight long years, and he may as well face the fact that he wasn't going to be able to do it now.

The door was slightly ajar, and as he raised his hand to knock he heard the sound of raised voices from inside the cottage.

'But I told you...'

'I know what you told me, darling, but it just wasn't true, was it?'

Louise's light tones and another, rougher, very masculine voice that he recognised instantly even after the length of time since he had last heard it.

Geoff Thornton.

The man he had once thought his friend but who had proved himself to be the exact opposite.

'Can't you give me another few days?'

Louise looked up into the disturbingly cold face of the man before her, quailing inside as she saw the ruthless cruelty stamped on it.

'You've had all the days you're getting! You pay by the end of the month or else.'

'But I told you — '

Three days ago she had hoped...but since then she hadn't seen or heard from Alex, and the one tiny chance of a solution that she had had seemed to have shrivelled into ashes, like paper in a flame, disintegrating totally.

 Tip: Spray air freshener behind radiators — it will disperse the smell for some time, and keep your home smelling lovely.

'Oh, I know what you said, darling. You made some ridiculous claim about being married — to Alex Alcolar, of all people! He'd sort this all out, you said. And quite frankly, I don't believe a word of it. If Alex is going to come riding to your rescue like a knight on a white charger, then he'd be here by now.'

'You told him! You wrote that letter!'

'I wrote — but nothing happened. If he's your husband, as you claim, then where the hell is he?'

'Here.'

The single word came from behind them both, making Thornton spin round in shock, a violent curse escaping his lips. Louise couldn't even manage that much. Though her mouth opened, no sound came out.

'Sorry I'm late, *querida*...'

Alex moved swiftly into the room, bypassing Thornton with only a coolly disdainful glance. Coming to Louise's side, he stunned her even further by dropping a swift, totally unexpected kiss on to her vulnerable mouth.

'I had a last-minute phone call just as I was leaving.'

If she had been capable of thinking of any reply, that kiss drove it totally from her mind. That and the use of that word, *querida*, along with the apparently genuine warmth in his tone made her head spin in disbelief. When he moved to her side and slid a strong arm around her waist, she welcomed its support with gratitude, her legs suddenly feeling as weak as cotton wool beneath her.

'So...'

At last he turned and surveyed the man before him, his slate-grey gaze cold and impenetrable.

'Shall we get down to business?'

'Alex...' Louise tried, but he silenced her with a smile and a swift shake of his head.

'No, *amada*...'

The softness of the words was threaded through with unyielding steel. A steel that was matched by the warning flash of those dark eyes, cautioning her not to overstep the invisible line he'd laid down.

'We agreed. I would deal with this. You can leave it to me. What I would like you to do is to make me a coffee. I'm parched...'

The none-too-subtle push he gave her left her no option but to head for the kitchen as he wanted. Any attempt to disobey would only result in an undignified struggle, one Alex would undoubtedly win with ease. So she gave in — for now.

She even made herself fill the kettle and switch it on. But the water boiled totally ignored as she struggled to listen to what was happening in the dining room.

The thickness of the door and the space of the hall between them blocked the words, so that all she could hear was the indistinct murmur of the two different voices, Thornton's loud and blustering, Alex's smooth and totally impassive. Louise found that she was clenching her hands tight in an attack of nerves, nails digging into her palms.

And then, just as she thought she couldn't bear it any longer, she heard the front door open and close on a loud and obviously angry slam. The next moment a car roared into life and sped away down the lane.

Alex or Thornton?

A swift glance out of the window gave her the answer. Alex's car was still parked opposite the cottage.

A rush of feeling swamped her, but even she couldn't have said whether it was relief or the opposite. Alex had got rid of Thornton, it seemed — but did that mean that she could say goodbye to all her problems, only to welcome in a whole new set of difficulties?

The phrase 'out of the frying pan and into the fire' sounded ominously inside her head as she forced her reluctant feet across the hallway to the dining room.

Alex was standing by the big open fireplace, staring down into the flames, a brooding expression on his stunning face. But he swung round as he heard the door open and Louise hesitated on the threshold.

'He's gone,' he said, anticipating her question. 'And he won't be back.'

'Can you be sure? How do you know?'

'I know,' Alex broke in curtly. 'He's had all the money that he's getting out of me, and I made it clear that if he tried anything again there was plenty of information that I could hand over to the police — information that could put him back inside if I chose to reveal it. Yes, you can be sure he's gone.'

'But that's wonderful!'

Impulsively she took a couple of steps forward, her hands coming out — then froze as she looked into his handsome face and saw the blank, opaque look in his eyes.

'He's gone,' he repeated. 'You're clear of him. Now you'll have to deal with me.'

CHAPTER FIVE

'I'll have to deal with you?'

Louise's heart jerked, seemed to stop, then lurched into a rough, unsteady beat. Nervously she swallowed hard.

What had Thornton told him? Just how much had the other man let slip? Oh, *why* hadn't she defied Alex's command and stayed in the room?

'What do I have to do?'

Once more Alex's smile was the opposite of warm.

'"Anything,"' he drawled. '"Just ask. If I can manage it, I'll do it."'

It took Louise a couple of shaken, bewildered moments to grasp just what he

meant. And when she realised that he was quoting her own words back at her, reminding her of her promise to do anything she could to thank him if he got Thornton off her back, her head spun in something close to real panic.

'You've — you've decided what you want.'

'I have.'

'And what is it?'

It was too late now to regret her rash promise. Too late to acknowledge that she had blundered in without thinking, and so landed herself between the devil and the deep blue sea. She had promised, and Alex had delivered the goods, so now she had to do the same.

'I want you to come back to Spain with me.'

'Spain?'

He couldn't mean it!

And even as she told herself that, she felt the sudden desperate rush of a longing for him to *really* want her to go to Spain with him. To be with him. As it had once been.

But, of course, that was not what he wanted.

'But I can't! I mean — I can't just walk out on things here. I have a job.'

'A job? As what?'

'I'm a nurse. In — in the premature baby unit in the local hospital.'

And that was coming way too close to memories that were painful even after all this time.

'A nurse? You?'

Suddenly, unexpectedly, the disbelief in his expression changed to something new and very different. There was a speculative light in his eyes as his cool grey gaze swept over her, a hint of a sexy grin curling the corners of his sensual mouth.

'I can just imagine you in the uniform...'

Louise's sigh was a blend of exasperation, relief and a hint of teasing amusement. At least this was safer ground.

'Don't tell me you're one of those guys who are turned on by the thought of a nurse's uniform. We don't wear the starched hats or the...'

Her voice faded, her throat drying, tension clutching at her heart.

The atmosphere in the room had changed, moving from calm, even relaxed, to nerve-tightening apprehension in the space of a heartbeat. But it wasn't fearful apprehension, more anticipation. A need. A longing.

'I wouldn't need a uniform to turn me on,' Alex said, and the same sensations that were tugging at her nerves were there in his voice, in the darkening of his eyes that held hers transfixed. 'You can do that all on your own. You always could. All I need is you.'

'Alex...'

'*Luisa*, come to me...'

And when he held out his hand it was as if he were a magician who had cast a spell over her. She couldn't resist, had no will to resist.

She didn't *want* to resist.

She wanted to be in his arms. It was the only place she had ever wanted to be. And as their warmth and strength closed around her it felt like coming home.

And then it didn't. Because Alex bent his head and took her mouth in a kiss that seared her soul. And then it felt as if she was venturing out into new and dangerous territory. But she knew she could never turn back. Because this was what she wanted. What she had missed so much in all those long lonely years.

'*Luisa...querida...amada*,' Alex muttered roughly against her mouth, and the words made her tremble in need.

She didn't care if he meant them or not. She only knew that they were part of the whirlwind of sensation that assailed her, and she needed them as she needed his kiss, the heat of his hands on her, smoothing, stroking, awakening the hunger that had always lain just below the surface whenever she was with him. She desperately wanted to feel the heat of his skin, and her fingers were clumsy with need as she tugged at the hem of the sweatshirt at his narrow waist.

With a rough laugh low in his throat, Alex helped her, shrugging off the soft material and coming back to her with the heat and hardness of his torso crushed against her upper body. And somehow he seemed to know that she so longed for him to follow suit and rid her of her own clothing, but he didn't put her out of her misery at once.

Instead he let those knowing, tormenting hands move everywhere. They slid under her sweater at the neckline, sending shudders of response right through her as his long fingers stroked the upper curves of her breasts, the sides. Then his hands moved away again to tangle tightly in her hair, pulling her face closer as he deepened and prolonged his kiss.

'Alex...' It was a moaning protest, a sound of impatience, and hearing it he soothed her gently.

'No rush, *querida*. We have all day...'

But, even as he spoke the words, Alex knew that he was deceiving himself.

No rush! Who was he kidding?

He might have wanted to take this slowly, but he knew it was impossible. From the moment that he had felt the softness of her body in his arms, the taste of her mouth on his and the scent of her skin in his nostrils, the hot and heavy pulse of desire through his body had taken over, pushing him to the edge of his control.

He skimmed the pink sweater from her in one swift movement and captured the warm weight of her breasts in his hands, cupping them through the flimsy lace that was their only covering. His thumbs stroked the delicate crests, rousing them to urgent hunger.

Louise moaned again, writhing against him, feeling the heat and hardness of his need for her against her hips. Her breath caught in her throat, her whole body stilling

as his mouth touched her shoulders, moved down, down, to close over one tight nipple, warm and demanding, his tongue tracing wildly erotic circles over her aching flesh.

'*Amada*...' His voice was raw and husky. 'Tell me, your bedroom is...?'

'Too far away. It would take too long. I want you here and now.'

Her tone was as rough as his. And as she spoke she was drawing him towards the open fire, drawing him down on to an old-fashioned rag rug before the hearth. On her knees before him, she tugged the fastening of his jeans free, slid the tight denim down the length of his legs and then made a raw, choking sound in her throat at the sight of his lean, muscled maleness in the firelight.

'Alex...' she muttered, and reaching out she closed her fingers around his hardness.

The soft touch shattered what little was left of his control. Pushing her back on to the rug, he came down on top of her, urgent hands lifting her skirt, tugging down the white lacy panties beneath it.

> **Tip:** Crumpled newspaper inside a handbag will help it keep its shape, and storing it in a pillowcase will make sure it stays in tiptop condition!

The flickering, changing light of the fire played out an endless succession of patterns on the pale limbs splayed beneath him, gilding his chest and arms, shadowing his face as he slid between her thighs, entering her on one long, slow, sensual thrust.

'I have waited so long for this,' he muttered against her yearning mouth. 'Too long. Far, far too long.'

'Too long...' she echoed on a broken sigh. But then as he moved inside her the sigh changed to a cry of delight, rising to a note of loss of control, and finally of total fulfilment as she lost herself completely in his arms.

And as she arched in total abandonment against him, Alex gasped out her name as he felt himself shatter in the hot, silken warmth of her body.

It was the start of a long, lingering, erotic afternoon. What they had begun by the heat of the blazing fire, they later continued, more slowly, in the deep, welcoming warmth of her bed. And as a result it was a long, long time before any sort of rational thought made its way back into Alex's mind.

But when, in the early hours of the morning, a degree of memory returned, it was the last words that Thornton had flung at him on the way out the door that slid coldly into his mind.

And made him wonder if he had made the worst mistake of his life.

CHAPTER SIX

Alex's home in Andalusia was quite the most beautiful place Louise had ever been to in her life.

But it was also the loneliest.

Even years ago when Alex had left the village and gone to take up his new life with his Spanish family, when she had found herself alone and pregnant, she had never felt as desolate as this. The closest she had come to this sense of desolation had been in those terrible days just after she had lost the baby — Alex's baby — and had felt that she would never know happiness again.

She had come to Spain because she'd had to. She knew now that she had never stopped loving Alex. Would never stop loving him. That first time she'd had to let him go because she'd had no alternative. But this time he had asked her to come with him. And after that day when they had made love she had known that it would kill her to let him walk out of her life again.

So she had annoyed the hospital by taking all the holidays she had available at the shortest possible notice. And she had come with him.

But something had changed. Alex was no longer the man he had been. The ardent, passionate lover seemed to have vanished, and in his place was a cold, withdrawn man. A man who no longer even seemed to want her. A man who hadn't even kissed her or touched her in the three days since they had arrived here.

He had made every effort to make sure that she was more than comfortable. Every need she had was met; every whim answered almost before she had a chance to express it. Every luxury that she might want, and some she had never even dreamed of, had been provided for her. But all that did was to emphasize how little Alex gave her *emotionally*.

And that lack of emotion was breaking her heart.

'*Luisa*? What are you doing? My family will

be here any minute.'

'I'm coming.'

She forced herself away from the window just as he pushed open the door and came into the room. And just the sight of him, his bronzed skin dark against the crisp white shirt, long legs sheathed in the black tailored trousers, was enough to make her heart jerk in uncontrolled response.

She loved him so desperately, but she had no idea how he felt about her — if, in fact, he felt anything.

'Is there something wrong?'

'Wrong? No.'

The lie brought stinging tears to her eyes so that his face blurred before her.

'Then why are you hiding yourself away up here?'

His tone was so sharp that she knew he wouldn't easily be distracted, that she would have to offer him some plausible explanation or he would never let the subject drop.

'All right then. If you must know, I'm nervous about meeting your father. He's given you so much...No?' she questioned as Alex shook his dark head angrily. 'But I assumed that your father...'

'Well then, you assumed wrong. My father gave me nothing but the start I wanted. The place at university. The position in his company where I could start out. Everything else I have I earned.'

That was so typically Alex that she couldn't hold back a small, soft smile. His pride would never have let him just have things given. Even though his father could well afford everything, he had to earn whatever came to him.

'What have you told him — and your brothers and sister — about why I'm here?'

What could he tell them? Alex wondered privately. How could he explain something that he didn't understand himself?

If he knew why she had come with him, things would be very different.

Or would they? Wasn't the truth of the matter the fact that he didn't want to know the answer, in case it turned out to be the opposite of what he'd hoped for?

'I've told them nothing,' he answered honestly. 'Nothing except that you are a visitor from England — someone I once knew.'

Someone I once knew. It had such a desolate sound to it. There seemed no hope of any future in those words.

'Did — did you tell them about the manor? About — ?'

'That's our secret. It's just between you and me.'

'I'll never be able to thank you, you know. If you hadn't come to my rescue, I don't know what I would have done.'

'Thornton certainly wanted more than I'd ever dreamed.'

Alex struggled to control his voice, keep the words even.

'Why didn't you tell me how bad things had got?'

'I — I didn't dare. To tell you the truth, I

couldn't believe it myself. Melissa must have been signing IOUs day and night. I knew I could never pay it. I was really beginning to think that I was going to be forced to take the only way out that Thornton had offered me...'

She shuddered expressively at just the thought.

'"The only way out".'

Alex pounced on the words like a tiger on its prey, bringing her up short in horror at the thought of what she had just inadvertently revealed.

'And what way was that? Louise!' he added warningly when she backed away, shaking her head in refusal to speak. 'Tell me!'

'I — I can't...'

'No,' he said grimly. 'But Thornton did. He wanted you to become his mistress. To pay him with sex. I almost killed him... I could still...'

'Please — no — it's over.'

Over for her, Alex admitted to himself, but now he had to live with what this news meant for him. He had paid Louise's debts for her. He had got her precious manor back, and had made sure that Thornton would never trouble her again.

And then he had taken her to bed.

He had done it because he loved her. Because in all the years they had been apart she had never truly been out of his thoughts. He had tried to forget her, but the truth was that he had never been able to.

And she had gone with him willingly. She had given herself to him without holding anything back.

But had she only done so because she felt it was the way that she could thank him? That, as Geoff Thornton had insinuated, this was the way she had expected to pay for her freedom, and all that had changed was the man to whom she owed the debt of gratitude?

His stomach heaved at the thought, and he couldn't bear to look into Louise's lovely face for fear of what he would see there. Instead, he whirled away, planning on heading for the door. On getting out of there before he said something that would give away what he was feeling.

But the suddenness of the movement created a whirling draught that caught some papers lying on the bed, lifting them and dropping them on to the floor.

'*Perdón*. I — '

Automatically he stooped to pick them up.

'No!'

Louise lunged forward, reaching desperately. But she was too late. Already those sharp grey eyes had scanned the first page. She saw him stop dead, flick a sudden, shocked glance in her direction, then go back and reread the page with a new and frightening intensity.

And she knew it was too late.

CHAPTER SEVEN

Alex read the letter through once more, then turned blazing eyes on Louise's ashen face.

'The Gabrielle Alcolar Memorial...Louise, what the hell *is* this?'

'It's...'

Twice she tried to answer. Twice her voice failed.

But she didn't really have to explain. Alex's swift, incisive brain had assessed the contents of the letter and come to the right conclusion.

'Gabrielle *Alcolar*. Were you pregnant? Did you have a child? *My* child?'

Louise could only nod miserably.

'And you didn't deign to *tell* me? To let me know...'

'She didn't live long enough for anyone to know her!' Louise burst in, tears flooding down her cheeks. 'She was born too early, and she died too early as well. She wasn't even a day old...'

'Oh, *Luisa*!'

Suddenly she was in his arms, her head pillowed on his chest, her tears soaking into his shirt.

And he just held her. Held her and let her weep, his voice murmuring soft, comforting words in gentle Spanish, as if in the emotion of the moment all his English had deserted him.

It was only when her sobs eased, when she drew in a deep, shuddering breath, that he put one hand under her chin and lifted her face so that her hazel eyes met the dark

intensity of his steely gaze, and shockingly saw the revealing glisten of his own tears in its depths.

'And this memorial — the home — this is what you wanted the manor for.'

Sniffing inelegantly, Louise managed to nod agreement.

'I wanted somewhere that mothers who had lost their babies this way could go. Somewhere they could have some time to recover, to convalesce. When Gabrielle died I spent hours just walking in the countryside around the manor, or reading in the library. I think it saved my life. I wanted others to have the chance, too.'

'I see.'

There was something in his voice that jarred. He was looking at the other document. The one that Louise knew was Gabrielle's birth certificate.

'You do understand. It was so very important to me.'

'Oh, yeah.'

He couldn't drag his attention away from the words that were on the paper in front of him. Gabrielle Louise Browning. Born 9 May. Gabrielle *Browning*. When his daughter's birth had been registered, she hadn't even been given his name.

'I see now how important the manor was to you.'

She'd lost him somehow, Louise realised. The long, lean body was stiff with rejection, held rigidly away from her.

Outside, the sound of a car pulling up alerted them to the fact that the first of their guests had arrived. Alex snatched at the excuse to escape.

'My family is here. I'll go down and let them in. You take the time you need. Come down when you're ready.'

But then, just as she managed a smile of thanks for his thoughtfulness, he drove it right away again with his next words.

'And don't worry about what they'll think of why you're here. I'll explain it's just for a short visit. Tell them that you're going home again tomorrow.'

It was not a suggestion but a command, Louise realised dazedly as the door swung shut behind him. He was *telling* her that she was going home again tomorrow. Dismissing her from his life — permanently, by the sound of it — and she didn't have the faintest idea why.

* * *

As Louise watched Alex's family drive away from the house, she felt her stomach tighten into hard, painful knots. She had been nervous at the thought of them arriving. Now she wished that they were staying for much longer.

Would Alex carry out his threat and send her home? Was he already wishing that she was gone?

But the man who walked ahead of her back into the cool tiled hallway was silent and withdrawn. She was going to have to be the one who opened the topic.

'I like your family,' she managed hesitantly. 'Your brothers are so like you. It's easy to see that you share the same father.'

Both Joaquin and Ramon Alcolar were every bit as tall, dark and stunning as their half-brother. But neither of them stirred her senses or made her feel the way the man before her did.

'And Mercedes...'

For the first time, Alex's face softened at the mention of his half-sister.

'Mercedes is a chatterbox,' he said. 'She never knows when to shut up.'

'It makes her easy to get on with.'

She prayed that the uneasiness in her mind didn't show in her voice. Mercedes had spent some time alone with her, and what Alex's sister had told her had unsettled her terribly. She had also found it impossible to believe.

'So...should I start packing?'

It was part question, part challenge. But Alex didn't respond to either.

'If I'm to leave tomorrow, I should... But, Alex, I don't want to go!'

That got a reaction from him. He had been heading into the kitchen, but now he whirled round. And something in his face, some shaken look in his eyes just before he managed to mask them again, told her that her comment had hit home.

But he covered his mistake quickly.

'Why not?' he asked coolly.

Not coolly enough, Louise decided. He had definitely been shaken. And that, combined with what Mercedes had said, gave her new determination. She was not about to be dismissed without at least a fight.

> 'I don't think I'm prepared to say — at least, not yet. Not until you've answered a question for me.'

It was there again. A tiny flash of wariness that, sensitive to everything about him, she caught where someone else might not.

'Louise, is this important?'

'Yes. I think so. It could be the most important thing I'll ever ask.'

She really had his attention now. Those slate-coloured eyes were fixed intently on her face, watching her closely.

'Then ask,' he said huskily.

CHAPTER EIGHT

Louise licked her painfully dry lips, wondering where to start.

Ask, Alex had said, giving her the chance she so desperately wanted. But now she was terrified that she would make a total mess of things if she didn't tread very carefully.

'Mercedes said — she said that you once told her something... She was teasing you, saying it was time you got married, and you told her that you'd already met the one woman who could ever be your wife.'

'Like I said, Mercedes talks too much.'

'But was she telling the truth?'

Her answer was there in his face. He didn't need to speak a word.

Louise's heart gave a little kick of excitement but she fought to keep calm. She wasn't out of the woods yet.

'That's what I told her.' Alex was clearly hedging his bets, too.

'And the woman? Who were you talking about?'

But she'd pushed him too far. His face changed, his jaw setting hard, and he shook his dark head violently.

'No. No more questions. It's my turn for some answers.'

'Ok, ask away.'

She hoped she sounded more confident than she felt.

'When Gabrielle — when our daughter was born — why...?'

'*I* didn't register her birth.'

She anticipated the question that was burning in his mind and answered without it needing to be asked.

'I didn't do it. I was too distressed to do anything. My father was the one who put the name Browning on the certificate.'

'But you were the one who called her Gabrielle Alcolar on the documents for the memorial home?'

He took her silence for the assent it was.

'Why? Because I was no longer plain Alex Anderson? No longer the housekeeper's son, but a member of the powerful Alcolar family? Because I could afford to buy...?'

'No! Oh, Alex, is that what you thought? Because if it was, then you couldn't have been more wrong. Your money — your position now — doesn't mean a thing to me.'

'No?'

The cynicism in his eyes stabbed at her like a knife.

'*No*! I always wanted Gabrielle to have her real name — your name. You were her father; she was your child. That was what mattered. If you'd read the letter properly — all the details — you'd have seen that the home was always going to have your name right from the start. Whether you helped me or not.'

'So the manor…'

'The manor is only a place. I wanted it to be a memorial to Gabrielle — to our child. But I wanted it to be named for you, too. Because…'

No. She didn't dare to admit that she loved him. Not yet. He still looked too wary, too unsure. She had to wipe away the scepticism, convince him somehow.

But how?

When inspiration struck suddenly, it was impossible to suppress a grin of pure delight. Impulsively she held out her hand.

'Alex, come with me.'

Alex eyed her suspiciously, wondering just what had put that glow on her face.

'What are you up to?'

'Please, trust me.'

When she turned those wide hazel eyes on him like that, and put the pleading note into her voice, then he would go with her anywhere. Do anything she asked. He couldn't stop himself.

And so he put his hand into hers and felt her soft fingers close around his.

She led him up the stairs and into a bedroom. *His* bedroom, not the separate single room where he had insisted that she sleep since their arrival at the house. Once there, she released him, left him standing in the middle of the room while she perched on the end of the big double bed.

'Louise, what…'

'No talking.'

She held up a hand to silence him.

'Just do as I say. Take your jacket off.'

For a second she thought he was going to refuse. But then suddenly he shrugged his broad shoulders, slid off the jacket and tossed it on to a nearby chair.

'And your shirt.'

He frowned his confusion, but surprisingly he obeyed her without a word.

'Now what, *señorita*?' Alex asked dryly, his attention totally focused on her. 'Don't tell me…'

Strong brown hands gestured, indicating the black leather belt at his waist.

'That's right.' The tightness in Louise's throat made her voice croak embarrassingly.

She expected rebellion, but surprisingly he obeyed her without a word. Perhaps something in her face had given her away. Perhaps he had sensed just how much this meant to her.

With the last garment of all, her nerve failed her. But Alex took the situation right out of her hands, stripping off the shorts to stand proud and unembarrassed in his nakedness before her.

'Isn't it about time you told me what all this is about, *querida*?'

Her heart thudding wildly, Louise got up from the bed and walked to stand beside him. With a hand that shook noticeably she reached out and touched him softly on the cheek, looking deep into his darkened eyes.

'Now you're what I want,' she said clearly, confidently. 'Now you're *all* I want — everything I want.'

'Not the money...?'

Where her voice had gained a new strength, Alex seemed to have lost some of his pride, his self-possession.

'Or the — '

'*Not* the money. Never the money. Not the manor or the name or anything...but you,' Louise assured him. 'You're what I need. Just you, nothing more. Just this one special man...'

'And you're all the woman I need. The only woman I want,' he told her. And to Louise, the words sounded the most wonderful she had ever heard in her life.

'Then will you answer my question?'

She didn't need to say which question. He knew exactly what she meant.

'Yes,' he said, his voice deep and husky with emotion. 'Yes, you were the one I told Mercedes about. Yes, you are the woman I love. The only woman I would ever want by my side. So please, *amada*, please tell me that you'll marry me and be my wife — for real, this time.'

'Oh, Alex, there isn't anything I'd love more in the whole world. Oh, yes...'

The words were silenced by his kiss. A kiss that promised the world and a glorious future together.

> **Tip:** Fill several small vases with fresh flowers and place them throughout your house — in the bathroom, on the bedside table, everywhere you spend time.

'Wife for real,' Louise echoed softly when he finally let her breathe again. 'Could anything be more perfect?'

'Just one thing,' Alex told her, his eyes gleaming silver with a blend of delight and need. 'But you have rather too many clothes on for what I have in mind.'

'I do, don't I?' Louise teased, joy lifting her voice, putting a bubble of laughter into it. 'Perhaps you'd like to help me with that?' ■

Watch out for Kate Walker's brand new Modern Romance **Spanish Billionaire's Innocent Bride** Available March 2008.

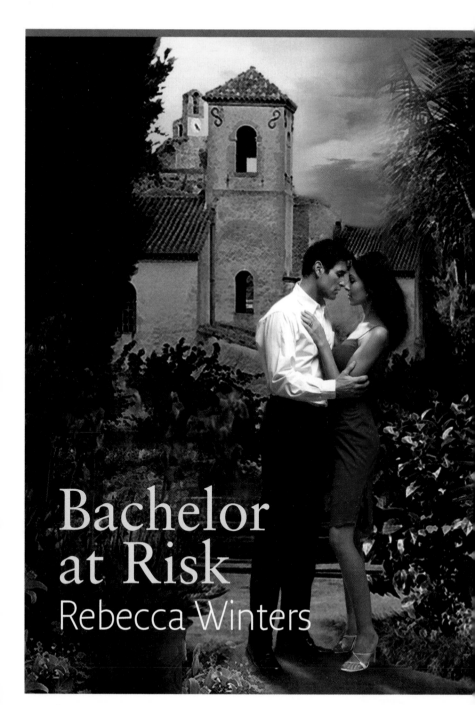

Bachelor
at Risk
Rebecca Winters

'Giselle?'

'Yes, Monsieur Armentier? How can I help?'

Jean-Jacques had only recently been installed as CEO of the Giraud Cosmetics Corporation, and since then his private secretary had shown him the greatest deference, but this business about calling him *Monsieur*, though well intentioned, was irritating the hell out of him. 'Couldn't you call me Jean-Jacques like you used to?'

'Are you sure?' She pretended to be scandalised, but he knew otherwise.

'I'm sure.'

Her chuckle sounded loud and clear over the speaker. 'I'm very happy to see that you're just the same.'

'When all is said and done, I'm still a mere chemist and the son of a flower farmer.'

'You're a lot more than that now!'

'Don't remind me. I've been told you're the one who normally walks around the complex on the last day giving out the Christmas bonuses.'

'That's right. Would you prefer that someone else did it?'

'Perhaps this one time you would allow me the privilege? I need an excuse to meet with everyone personally before they go home for the holiday. If I'm handing out money, they might just return after New Year.'

Giselle's chuckle turned into full-bodied laughter. 'The cheques are in the safe, all ready for your signature.'

'Wonderful. I've been thinking it might be nice if they were to receive their bonuses today instead of Wednesday.'

'You must have read my mind,' she quipped. Then, on a more serious note, she added, 'If you want to know the truth, everyone is happy you've been put in charge.'

Jean-Jacques cleared his throat. 'That's good to hear, but I'm still not sure this isn't a dream. Any minute now I expect to wake up flat on my back in a lavender field just waiting to be harvested.'

'Now you have to worry about the entire company instead of one flower farm. I'll be right in with the cheques.'

By the end of the day he'd delivered envelopes to everyone in the building except Vivige Honfleur, a woman he hadn't yet met. She ran the day care centre, which was a recent innovation. Five years ago, before Jean-Jacques had left Vence to get his degree and work for the Giraud perfumery in Paris, the centre hadn't existed. As far as he was concerned, it was a terrific and much-needed addition to the workplace.

Hopefully the working parents with children had already picked up their offspring, and he'd be able to talk to Madame Honfleur without distraction. He walked out the front doors to the modern facility adjacent to the car park, recalling how pleased the workers had been to receive their Christmas bonuses early. Many of them had taken the time to renew their acquaintance with him — and he was glad he had recognised so many of them.

Several mothers he'd spoken with earlier in the day were leaving with their toddlers. They chatted for a minute before he moved inside to the day care.

Voices carried from one of the rooms set up like a class with tables, chairs and toys. Jean-Jacques walked through the doorway where he saw a curly-headed toddler talking to his teacher while she helped him on with his coat.

A man swept past him to collect his child, but Jean-Jacques's attention was suddenly riveted to the stunning woman who stood up to greet the boy's father, smoothing her skirt, which had ridden up one gorgeous, shapely leg where the child had been clutching her.

Mon Dieu. It was Nicole.

> ❄ **Tip:** For a stress relieving bath, add three cups of chamomile tea to your bath water. Chamomile has soothing, healing properties that ease away tension.

Like the flowers that made up his world, Nicole Giraud, heiress to the Giraud perfume fortune, had always been an integral part of it. From their youth, her sweet nature, not just her beauty, had worked its way into his blood. Nicole and Provence. The two were inseparably connected.

If he hadn't known she was getting married right away and going to live in England, he would never have considered returning to Vence as CEO. It had been five years since he'd seen her. Yet looking at her

now made it seem like yesterday.

Nicole said goodbye to little Luc, then turned to the other waiting parent. 'May I help — '

She didn't finish what she was going to say because it wasn't another father who'd come into the room, looking taller and leaner than she'd remembered. Though she tried to quell it, a soft gasp escaped her throat. '*Jean-Jacques...*'

She'd known this moment had to come some time, but she still wasn't prepared for it. His black eyes that used to pierce through to her very soul before kissing her into oblivion had developed a brooding quality. As they travelled over her features, she could find no trace of warmth in their assessing regard. There wasn't even a hint of the gentle, teasing side of his nature, which used to melt her bones.

'It's been a long time, *chérie*,' he finally responded with enviable calm and a certain emotional detachment that made her heart drop to the floor like a stone.

The intervening years — the years he'd left her and been in Paris — had wrought changes. His olive skin wasn't as bronzed as it used to be. Of course that was only natural as he hadn't worked in the fields for years now. He'd become a man with a man's aloofness.

Physically he was more attractive to her than ever. He still wore his dark hair a little longer than was currently fashionable, tempting her to run her fingers through it.

But there were new lines of experience around his nose and mouth, giving him a harder edge. His very remoteness challenged her to break through the veneer to find the man she'd lost her heart to years before.

Standing this close to him again, she realised that nothing had changed for her. If anything she was even more in love with him.

'You haven't changed, Nicole. You're still the beautiful girl who used to drop by my father's plant to give me a thrill when you didn't have something else more important to do with your time.'

Nicole snapped her head back, dislodging the rich brown hair from her shoulders. Until he'd said that, she'd never known he had a problem with their different backgrounds. How strange to think he'd even considered there was a class barrier between them. She had been too caught up in her feelings for him to even consider their differences.

'If you recall, your father's plant was the first place I went to every day after school for years because I knew you'd be there. It was the only place I wanted to be,' she confessed in a quiet voice.

Jean-Jacques lifted his shoulders in that elegant yet careless shrug so typical of him, before straightening. In an instant his features had taken on a chiselled cast. 'That was a long time ago.'

'A very long time ago.' It was impossible to keep the tremor out of her voice.

'I must admit I'm surprised to find you here at the day care centre of all places.'

She took a deep breath. 'It was built the year you left Vence. Every December since then I've worked with the children to enact the nativity scene for the Christmas Eve programme.'

The news stunned him. He shifted his weight. 'Isn't that a fairly ambitious project when you're planning to get married so soon?'

Nicole's lambent brown eyes searched his with a frankness that gave his heart another dangerous workout. 'You mean to Colin?'

Jean-Jacques rubbed the back of his neck. 'If you're referring to the Englishman I saw you with in the papers, then I suppose yes. It said something about an impending holiday wedding. I didn't really take note of the rest.'

A stillness emanated from her. 'No, we're not getting married.'

Jean-Jacques froze. He couldn't have heard correctly. If Nicole wasn't getting married, what would it mean for them...?

CHAPTER TWO

'You mean you're not getting married at Christmas?' Jean-Jacques needed to be perfectly clear on what Nicole meant.

She paused in the process of straightening the chairs. 'I mean, I was never going to be married. It's true I was in London recently to represent my mother at a family party. Some photographer caught me out on the lawn talking to Colin. He's marrying his fiancée in a few days.'

With those words, Jean-Jacques's entire world turned inside out. She wasn't engaged...There wasn't going to be a marriage...She wouldn't be living in England...*Mon Dieu.*

He'd imagined many things since he'd seen the photograph. All of them gut-wrenching.

He fought to smother a groan. 'My mistake. I was about to offer my congratulations.'

An impish smile broke out on her face. 'It appears you've joined a long line of people duped by the paparazzi.'

When she looked like that, she had no idea how she came across to the males of the species. It was something she did as naturally as breathing. He'd known her since she was a little girl with a mop of bouncing curls. Her charm had got beneath his skin then, and would always have a stranglehold on his heart.

Now that she'd grown into a breathtaking woman, it didn't surprise him that every journalist in Europe wanted photographs of her. Heiress to the Giraud perfume fortune, he supposed she would always be hounded by the press.

'Guilty as charged,' he replied in the same teasing vein to disguise his shock.

She moved closer to him, her eyes intent on his face. 'I never imagined such a thing could happen to Jean-Jacques Armentier of all people. Not when you used to laugh with me over the ridiculous claims in the tabloids linking me to this prince and that shipping magnate. Remember?'

Oh, yes. I remember. How I wish I didn't. For the love of heaven, Nicole, don't look at me like that.

It was the same way she used to look at him whenever he tried to play hard to get. He did it on purpose to gauge her reaction. Her eyes would glisten over in pain and she'd go all breathless. Every time she responded that way, it would prove that she wanted him as much as he wanted her.

Something dark in his nature had always needed that proof because he couldn't believe that Nicole Giraud, the exquisite brunette men all over Europe fantasised about, the daughter of a family worth billions, would rather be with *Jean-Jacques Armentier*, a son of the soil who was very good at entertaining her but could never be her equal.

No matter how many times he'd tested her, she'd still come after him, undaunted. In front of his peers her unswerving desire for him had fed his inflated ego. In the privacy of night, with the taste of her mouth still on his, he felt his heart soar. Then the morning would come, when the harsh light of day had brought reality, dashing every dream.

How jealously he'd guarded her all those years. Right up until the moment he'd left for Paris with an offer that had settled an untenable situation for him. But that had been a lifetime ago.

His jaw hardened. This conversation

needed to end so that the torture would end. 'If you're not getting married, what is the favourite target of the paparazzi doing these days besides putting on a Christmas play?'

Tell me what I need to hear. Tell me you're planning a world cruise with your lover. Anything that puts thousands of miles between us.

Nicole was in so much pain over his indifference to her presence, she didn't know if she could answer him. The question he'd asked her had been motivated by courtesy, nothing more. It went to prove how totally he'd eradicated her from his consciousness.

'Brigitte never mentioned it?'

'I'm afraid my sister and I were both poor letter writers,' came the dampening response.

Her heart plunged to new depths. Not only had Jean-Jacques been able to steal away in the night five years ago and abandon everything and everyone he knew without a backward glance, he hadn't shown enough curiosity to ask questions of his older sister who'd been a good friend to Nicole.

There'd been no concern on his part about how she'd survived that empty black period of endless mourning.

Devastated hadn't begun to describe Nicole's feelings at the time. One day he had been working at his father's plant where the harvested lavender was processed. The next day Jean-Jacques had been gone. With

obvious pride Monsieur Armentier told Nicole his son had left for Paris to study chemistry.

He'd never written to her. Never phoned. There'd been no explanation. *Dear God*. The pain had been so excruciating she still hadn't recovered, and feared she never would.

'I've been doing what I always intended to do with my life when I grew up.'

Her reply managed to wipe the faint mocking expression from his face. In its place crept a sober mask, realigning those attractive features.

'You're a *teacher*?'

The fact that he remembered even that much of past conversations ought to have brought her a modicum of solace. But his glaring incredulity didn't allow her one second's pleasure in the moment.

She fought not to let him see how devastated she was. In as level a tone as possible she said, 'I've been instructing kindergarten children for four years now.'

'Where?' he asked.

'At the École Charles Martel.'

He flashed her an impatient glance. 'I meant "where" as in which town?'

'Here in Vence, of course. I was thrilled to be assigned that school because it's only a few minutes from the office. My brother and I were able to enjoy many lunches together before he moved to New York.'

She could have sworn his face lost colour.

'But that's impossible...'

'Why?' she burst out angrily. 'Is it so unthinkable that a Giraud might be teaching at the same school an Armentier attended?'

'You misunderstand me, Nicole,' he ground out. 'To be frank, I hadn't imagined you — '

'Working at all?' she cut him off. 'Having a job like an ordinary person? For someone who always seemed so down-to-earth, you have a real problem about people with money. I don't know how I failed to recognise it until now — '

His mouth thinned into a white line of anger, but she didn't care. She was just getting warmed up.

'I'm not sure you'll be able to handle what I'm going to tell you, Jean-Jacques, but I'll say it anyway. All those billions you're now responsible for have *never* had anything to do with me. I didn't earn as much as one cent! The only money I spend is what I make on my salary.'

It was fascinating to watch the way his black eyes turned into furious pinpoints of light.

'Impossible as it is for you to believe, money doesn't make my world go round.'

Her declaration reverberated in the room. The way Jean-Jacques was staring at her now made her realise how out of control she was sounding.

'The children here at the day care centre,' she began in a quieter tone, 'will be presenting the Christmas play at the villa. Mother's planning a light supper for everyone on the staff. She sent an invitation to your office, but in case you haven't seen it yet, I'm extending it personally.'

A long silence ensued before he said,

'Giselle already brought it to my attention. Please, thank your mother for me.'

'I will,' she whispered. 'Does that mean you're coming?'

CHAPTER THREE

Would he attend the Christmas party at her mother's home?

Jean-Jacques realised it was like it had been before — Nicole standing there with those velvety-brown eyes beseeching him for an answer.

'I've already asked Giselle to accept your mother's invitation for me. Now, if you'll excuse me, I must look up Madame Honfleur's address and drop off her bonus.'

Anxious to put distance between himself and Nicole, Jean-Jacques pulled out his car keys.

'She lives above her husband's shop,' Nicole said before he'd reached the door. 'It's the *bureau de tabac* at the base of the rue Madelaine bordering the Place de Seurat. You know wh-where you and I used to buy chocolates on our way to the beach.' She stammered the last.

Jean-Jacques wished she hadn't mentioned those marshmallow delights covered in chocolate. They'd take a sack of them to an isolated stretch of sand and water to watch the yachts in the distance. But he never had seen anything except the invitation in her beguiling smile. There was nothing sweeter than her lips covered in orange, mint and raspberry.

Even now they were a temptation he could do without.

Auguste Giraud had seen what was happening between his daughter and the boy who was completely unsuitable for her. For years he'd watched and waited until the exact moment to proffer the bribe that had sent Jean-Jacques out of his daughter's life.

Little did her father know that Jean-Jacques had already made plans to leave the Midi, the South of France region in which Vence was located. At twenty-five he had been a man, hot with a man's desire, unable to bear the torture of her presence when he hadn't been able to do anything about it. But he wasn't certain that, at some point, he wouldn't break his own vow and come running back to her. Lyon wasn't that far from Vence.

The bribe to go all the way to Paris had been presented to him when he was at his most vulnerable. So many miles between them guaranteed that he wouldn't backslide and come back to Vence every weekend.

Until he'd found out Nicole wasn't getting married after all, Jean-Jacques had actually believed he was home free. Now everything he'd strived so carefully to orchestrate had blown up in his face.

As soon as he made his delivery to Madame Honfleur, he'd go back to his apartment and phone Dominic Giraud in New York. Nicole's older brother was the one who'd picked Jean-Jacques to be CEO. It was to Dominic he would tender his resignation.

Hopefully a replacement could be found and installed by the first of the year.

> **Tip:** Rings and earrings can be cleaned by soaking in undiluted washing-up liquid for a few minutes. Then just rinse and shine with a soft cloth.

'Thank you for the information. *À bientôt,* Nicole.' He left, determined to keep as far away from her as possible. If he worked his schedule correctly, there was no reason for him to see her again. He ignored the sinking feeling that thought gave him.

* * *

Long after Jean-Jacques had left the room, Nicole stood there trembling. Something was wrong. If her instincts were correct, and she had every reason to believe they were, he was afraid of being alone with her. Why? It made no sense, not after the history they'd shared.

Dear God, they'd known each other since childhood! For as long as she could remember life, Jean-Jacques had been part of the mosaic making up her world. At first as one of the older boys who had teased and sometimes played with her while her father had visited Jean-Jacques's father at the *lavanderie.* Later, as the heartthrob teenager she idolised long before she'd grown up enough to feel physical desire and express it.

By her mid-teens they'd begun to share an intense personal relationship. In time she realised he was the man she wanted to be her husband and the father of their babies. He'd wanted her, too!

He may not have said the words. He may not have made any commitments, but she'd known the depth of his feelings every time he'd crushed her in his arms, every time he'd devoured her mouth with an unrestrained hunger that had matched her own. Too unrestrained for him to behave around her now as if she were nothing more than an old acquaintance.

Even if his feelings for her had died five years ago, prompting his sudden departure from Vence, how could he pretend an indifference that simply didn't ring true?

If he thought he'd had the last word, he was very much mistaken. She was tired of not having answers. He owed her an explanation. She was desperate for closure so she could get on with the rest of her life. Now that he'd been brought back to Vence to run the company, she wasn't about to waste another second torturing herself over the past.

Wheeling around, she locked up the day care centre and headed for her car. Tomorrow wasn't that far away. Never before had she deliberately used her name to get something she wanted — not from Jean-Jacques or anyone else. But there was always a first time...

Starting in the morning, she planned to fight for him any way she could.

* * *

'Jean-Jacques?'

'Yes, Giselle?'

'Nicole Giraud is here to see you.'

Jean-Jacques broke out in a cold sweat. It was one thing to be able to walk away from her yesterday. But it was quite another to refuse to see Nicole in his office when it was her family's money paying his salary.

Damn Dominic Giraud for being unavailable. His voice mail indicated he'd gone on vacation and wouldn't be back until the first of the year. All Jean-Jacques could do was leave a message that he'd made a mistake accepting the position, requesting a meeting with Dominic at his earliest convenience because he was handing in his resignation.

'Tell her to come in, Giselle.'

He steeled himself not to respond. But the moment she walked inside and shut the door, the sight of her in a stylish cherry-red wool dress took his breath. Her brunette colouring, combined with her voluptuous body and long slender legs made it impossible to look anywhere else.

After a lifetime of seeking him out at one of the flower farms or the *lavanderie*, it must be quite a shock for her to have to come to her brother's former office in order to talk to him.

'Thank you for fitting me in. I know you're busy.' She sounded a little breathless as she sat down in one of the chairs opposite his desk. He attributed the heightened colour in her cheeks to the cold weather outside.

'You're always welcome, Nicole. You know that. What can I do for you?' He tried to sound as if he were addressing a member of the board of directors.

Mon Dieu. Her eyes always had that expectant look when they met his, as if she were excited to see him. Five years had changed nothing in that regard! But no degree or title could alter the fact he was still an Armentier. They were adults now. There were certain lines you didn't cross. Nicole had always been out of reach, and always would be. The sooner he left Vence for good, the better.

When her brother demanded an explanation for this sudden about-face, Jean-Jacques would tell him the truth. That he was, and always had been, in love with Nicole. Dominic was a man and understood these things. Once he'd heard that revelation, he'd accept Jean-Jacques's resignation without question.

'With the establishment of the day care centre, Dominic and I started a tradition at the villa of giving presents to the children after their performance. We shopped together for their gifts and had a lot of fun doing it. I guess you've inherited that job now.'

He groaned inwardly. For years he and Nicole had gone Christmas shopping for their families' and friends' gifts. On their last Christmas together, before he'd made the decision to leave Vence, he'd wanted to take her to a jeweller's and let her pick out an engagement ring.

But that was one of those fantasies no one else knew about, least of all Nicole. He didn't have the kind of money to buy a ring she could be proud of. Of course it was absurd to even entertain the idea when marriage to her was out of the question.

'With Christmas Eve only three days away, the gifts really should be bought today.'

Dominic had forgotten to go over this duty with him. Come to think of it, he'd forgotten to tell Jean-Jacques several things...all having to do with Nicole.

'Giselle said you don't have a business lunch scheduled, so I thought we could grab a bite to eat, then run over to Toy World. But, of course, if you're too involved in something else...'

Nicole looked at him, her eyes bright and challenging, as if she was daring him to spend time with her. But that couldn't be right...or could it?

CHAPTER FOUR

Nicole's request was something Jean-Jacques couldn't turn down, otherwise it would make the situation appear to take on more importance than it warranted.

'How many children are there?' he asked to prevent her from leaving. She was already on her feet.

'Forty, if you count the babies and toddlers. Only the four- and five-year-olds will be coming to the villa. There are eighteen of them.'

Maybe it would be better to just get it over with now. Then he would only have to see her on Christmas Eve and that would be the end of it. Depending on how soon Dominic returned his call, Jean-Jacques could be back in Paris by New Year's Day.

'I have a phone conference arranged for two o'clock, but can fit in the shopping as long as we skip lunch.'

'That's fine with me,' she said, sounding undaunted. 'Now that my students are out of school for the holidays, I've had a big breakfast with my parents the last two mornings.'

He followed her to the outer office, where she reached for her coat. Then they headed for the company car in the car park.

'I thought you had a leisurely breakfast with your parents just about every morning.' He shut her door, then went around to the driver's side of the car.

Nicole waited until they were merging with the traffic. 'That might have been true when I was little. But like you, Jean-Jacques, I grew up and moved out of my parents' house years ago.'

 Fact: The Queen's Christmas speech was televised for the first time in 1957

Where? A tight band around his chest constricted his breathing. As long as she'd lived at her parents' villa, she'd been like the princess on the glass hill. You needed a magic horse to ride to the top to claim her. There was nothing magic about the plough horses in the Armentier barn. They would never fill the bill...

'Does that mean you're living in Antibes now? It's very beautiful along that stretch of the coast,' he said, remembering a time when they'd been riding around the towns near Vence on his motorbike and she'd pointed out the spectacular home overlooking the water, indicating that her father's aged parents lived there.

'Antibes...'

'Yes. Didn't you move into the villa your grandfather left to you?'

Nicole let out an angry laugh. 'My grandparents' home was meant to be filled with a family, not a single working woman. I rent a small studio apartment down on the rue de Mistral.'

His heart slammed into his ribs. It wasn't very far from his own apartment. He didn't want to hear any more. He didn't want to think about her there, alone, where he could have easy access.

'You amaze me, Jean-Jacques.' Her voice trembled. 'Do you honestly imagine that I lie around in some obscenely expensive designer negligee on my private terrace overlooking the Mediterranean while I sip champagne and contemplate how I'm going to spend my billions this weekend?'

When he had been in his late teens, those had been his exact thoughts, only they hadn't stopped there. He'd visualised himself climbing up to her terrace and making slow, passionate love to her beneath the Midi sun, their bodies caressed by a gentle breeze filled with the scent of jasmine.

A deep ache seared him at the memory. Shakespeare could have set his two star-crossed lovers in Provence. Their names, Armentier and Giraud. Auguste Giraud wasn't the only person who'd wanted the two of them permanently separated. Jean-Jacques's parents had been equally adamant on the subject of their son ending all association with Nicole.

'It seems a great deal has changed while

I've been away. I promise to stop making any more assumptions.' He turned sharply to the right into the covered parking of Aux Quatre Saisons department store. 'It may take a while for me to find a parking space. Why don't I let you out here and meet you in the toy department?'

To his relief, she didn't object. 'See you a minute,' she said, before getting out of the car.

While he waited for the vehicle in front of him to move on, his eyes followed every bewitching movement of her gorgeous body. All the Christmas shoppers were watching her, too. Nicole was Vence's own unofficial princess. She couldn't go out in public without being the centre of attention.

Mon Dieu, Nicole. I shouldn't have come with you. Already I have this gut feeling I'm going to regret it...

* * *

The second Nicole entered the store, she expelled the breath she'd been holding. For a moment back in his office, she'd been afraid Jean-Jacques would refuse to come with her. But just because he'd felt obliged to help with the shopping, it didn't mean she could get him to do anything else.

Deep in her heart, she knew it was going to take some kind of miracle to get back what they'd once had.

With a determination born of her love for him, she proceeded with her plan. By the time Jean-Jacques joined her in the girls'

section of the toy store, she'd already ordered mobiles for the babies and push toys for the toddlers to be wrapped and sent to the day care centre.

Her pulse raced the moment she saw his tall, dark figure stride down the aisle towards her. Even from the distance separating them, she felt his black eyes searching hers. In his tan business suit, he looked every inch the urbane CEO, yet every woman in the store was aware of his hard-muscled body, the way it moved with that swift male grace of which he was unaware.

Gathering three of the season's most popular dolls in her arms, she turned so Jean-Jacques could see them. 'Which face do you like the best?'

Through shuttered lids, his gaze passed over her face and body with haunting thoroughness before he fastened his attention on the dolls she was holding.

His dark brows furrowed. 'They're not very appealing.'

She chuckled. 'I know. They're supposed to be homely. That's what makes them so endearing. Every little girl in France wants one. They're all the rage. Help me pick.'

'I'm afraid you've asked the wrong person. If Brigitte had owned a doll like that, I probably would have hidden it just to give her a hard time.'

'That's a terrible thing to say.' But she smiled as she said it. 'A lot of help you're being.'

'I guess the redhead isn't so bad. Maybe you'd better give every girl the identical doll so they won't fight. The same ought to go for the boys.'

'Have you decided on a gift for them?'

'Of course. A toy car, preferably a red Ferrari like your father's. Every little boy's fantasy.'

If he'd proffered that little jab to remind her that they came from different worlds, it wasn't going to work. 'Terrific! That made our shopping easy. I'll tell the sales clerk to get everything wrapped and have the gifts sent to the villa.'

Before long they were back in the car trying to exit the shopping area, but the crowds were worse than ever. She heard Jean-Jacques mutter something unintelligible as he was forced to start, then stop, while they waited for the line of cars to move.

'We should have come on your motorbike.' With her heart thudding in her chest, she ventured, 'Do you still have it?'

'I would imagine it's still in my parents' garage.'

'After you're through at the office for today, why don't we go for a ride on it?'

Lines darkened his face. 'All right, Nicole. It's obvious you didn't need my help to buy toys. What was your real motive for getting me to come with you today? The truth,' he bit out tersely.

She swallowed hard. 'Five years ago you left Vence without one word of goodbye to me. Considering that I probably spent more time with you growing up than I did my own family or friends, it came as a tremendous shock to drive up to the *lavanderie* and be told you weren't there, that you'd left for Paris and wouldn't be coming back.'

There was a tremor in her voice that touched something deep inside of him.

'Obviously you were so excited to leave, you gave no thought to anything else. It didn't even occur to you to write a note that you could have asked your family to pass on to me. Had you grown to despise my company so much you couldn't spare me five minutes' explanation?'

Nicole turned to face him as Jean-Jacques decided what to say. Could he tell her the truth?

CHAPTER FIVE

The tension in the car was explosive as Nicole waited for Jean-Jacques to tell her why he had left without a word all those years ago.

He surrendered the parking slip to the attendant and pulled out into the traffic before attempting to respond. It was a question for which he'd had no satisfactory answer five years ago, so he'd done the cowardly thing and had left Vence without facing her.

But just now he'd heard in her demand an underlying bleakness that he didn't want to acknowledge, yet couldn't ignore. Only Nicole had the power to slip past his defences and tie him in knots.

'Long before I went away, I'd been wrestling with the decision to do something more with my life than grow flowers,' he began.

'How come you never told me?'

'Until I'd worked out a plan, it wasn't something I wished to discuss with anyone.'

Her head was bowed. 'I lived in a fantasy world back then, didn't I? Imagining that I knew everything going on inside of you?'

'Does one human being ever really know another?'

'You knew me!' she blurted with raw emotion.

He sucked in his breath. 'I knew you were a Giraud, Nicole. You were also very young.'

Her head swerved in his direction. 'Why don't you say what you really mean — that I was a naïve little fool.'

'You're putting words in my mouth. I meant that you weren't old enough to know what life would present to you one day. Though you've always played it down, you were born to a world of privilege that only a handful of people will ever experience.'

'What does that have to do with anything?' she cried out angrily. 'Every person is born to a world unique to them. But just because my father makes more money than yours shouldn't have any bearing on our relationship. You make it sound as though we come from different planets.'

'I'm not so sure that isn't the right analogy.' He felt her gaze penetrate to his soul.

'I can't believe what I'm hearing! Up until the day you disappeared, I don't recall those differences preventing you from spending every free moment with me.'

'It was always in private, Nicole. I was no more welcome in your home than you were in mine.'

'That's not true!' she fired back. 'I begged you to come to my house and spend time with me. I could never understand why you refused. Neither could Mother. But until just now I had no idea your family didn't approve of me.' Her voice broke.

Oh, hell. He raked an unsteady hand through his hair. 'It wasn't a case of disapproval. I knew they'd be uncomfortable. That's why I didn't invite you.'

'Uncomfortable!' she cried. 'Why?' Her incredulity made him realise she honestly didn't know. Nicole had always been blind to colour and class differences. Those were just a few of the traits he loved about her.

He shook his head. 'If you don't understand it by now, then heaven help me, I can't explain it to you. It's a moot point anyway. To explain what happened — an unexpected opportunity came my way to study in Paris, so I took it.'

'Did some benefactor give you money?' The tears in her voice tore at his soul.

He was skirting dangerous ground now. 'Yes. It was like a miracle. For the first time in my life I could look down the road at the possibility of a different future. But it meant leaving my parents who needed me, though they would deny it.'

It meant leaving you, he added in his mind. *Looking at you right now, I don't know how I found the strength.*

'You couldn't have told me that much in a note at least?'

By now they were getting close to the

office. 'Nicole — do you remember the day you told me you wished I didn't smoke, and dared me to stop?'

'Yes,' came the quiet reply. 'You stubbed it out and never smoked again.'

'Leaving home was like throwing that last cigarette away. It was all or nothing. If I'd started with the goodbyes, I would never have left. Before I lost my courage, I packed my things and headed for the train while the family was still asleep.'

A prolonged silence filled the interior of the car. He turned into the car park and pulled to a stop near the main doors of the building.

Her lovely features looked frozen in marble. 'Thank you for telling me the truth. All these years I — I thought you must have hated me. Now I realise that the day you left, you chose to put away childish things.' After another hesitation, she added, 'Did you love Paris?'

Get out of the car now, Armentier. Otherwise you know what you're going to do, and then Nicole will be in no doubt of your feelings for her.

He forced a smile. 'Does a Frenchman love the sun?' After turning off the engine, he pulled the keys from the ignition, ready to exit the car.

She lifted tremulous brown eyes to him. 'Jean-Jacques? I know you have a phone conference in a minute, but would you do me a favour? It's the last one I'll ever ask of you.'

Adrenaline surged through his body as he realised she was prepared to say goodbye. 'If I can.'

'I'm giving a small cocktail party tonight. Would you drop by my apartment for drinks? Consider it a welcome home present from an old friend who was robbed of the pleasure of giving you a proper send-off. Any time after eight o'clock. I live at number 14, rue de Mistral.'

She looked at him rather sadly and smiled. Then she shut the car door behind her before he could answer.

* * *

Nicole hovered near the front window of her apartment, worried because Jean-Jacques hadn't arrived yet. She looked around the tiny living room decorated with a small Christmas tree and red poinsettias. It was almost nine o'clock. The hors d'oeuvres would have to be reheated.

With every passing minute she had to wait, her temperature rose another degree. The tension made even the sleeveless black mandarin silk dress feel too hot for her.

Her heart gave a furious kick when she heard footsteps outside the door, then a knock. She opened it to meet his unsmiling regard.

There was a forbidding look about him tonight. She wondered at her temerity in asking him to her home. Swallowing hard, she said, '*Bonsoir*, Jean-Jacques. I'm so glad you could make it. Come in.'

'*Merci.*' In a few swift strides he moved past her, careful not to brush against her arm. As she was closing the door, she caught him appraising her with the kind of thoroughness that had always taken her breath in the past. *Take a good look, my love*, she thought. *I'm no longer a child you can dismiss like you did five years ago.*

If he were as immune to her as he'd led her to believe earlier today, he wouldn't have come over tonight. Overjoyed at this much progress, she stared back at him. Few men were as naturally elegant as Jean-Jacques. Tonight his formal navy suit and paisley tie gave him the air of a successful business tycoon.

In her childhood she'd been too young to articulate what she'd found so attractive about him. By her teens the word dashing had come to mind. When she'd turned twenty, he was captivating. Everything about him had fascinated her.

But six years had added another element. He now had the irresistible appeal of a virile male who'd outgrown all traces of the younger man. She was staggered by his sensuality.

'I hope you're hungry. Please, sit down and help yourself to my home-made eggnog while I get the appetisers from the kitchen.'

He remained where he was, his stance formidable. His black eyes had narrowed on her mouth. 'Where are the rest of your guests?'

CHAPTER SIX

Nicole braved Jean-Jacques's piercing glance. 'There are no other guests.'

'Why did you allow me to think otherwise?'

'Because I knew you wouldn't come unless I told you there would be other people.'

He cursed. 'Damn you, Nicole! You got me over here under false pretences.' A dull red had crept beneath the skin of his handsome face. 'We covered everything that needed to be said in the car.'

She didn't move a muscle. 'But I didn't have my Christmas present for you with me then.'

> **Tip:** If you want to welcome guests with that great baking smell but you don't have time to whip something up, why not pop a part-baked baguette from your local supermarket in the oven?

His lips thinned in a hard line. 'I suppose that's as good an excuse as any for a private talk about my new position with the company. But your effort isn't necessary. I know I could never fill your brother's shoes. We both know that would be an impossibility.'

'That's not true,' she said, wounded by his aggressive attack as the last thing she doubted about him was his business abilities.

'Tell that to someone who doesn't know you as well as I do,' he said with maddening calm. 'You always were a highly emotional woman. Why don't you save all that charged energy for someone who would believe you?'

Nicole shook her head. 'Why are you being

like this?' More than ever she was convinced his uncharacteristic rudeness hid something he didn't want her to see.

'You think I don't know you have a right to be upset?' The cords stood out in his neck. 'Unfortunately it's a *fait accompli*. All I can do is make certain the comptroller of the company sends you monthly statements and keeps you apprised of developments as they occur.'

'That won't be necessary.'

'No one has more right to information than you.' He kept talking as if she hadn't said a word. 'One day half of the Giraud fortune will belong to you. I promised your brother I would protect and hopefully increase those holdings. I make you the same promise.'

'Fine, but I was never in any doubt of it.' She moved away from him and reached under the tree for his present.

He backed away from her. 'I don't have time for this.'

'Surely you have a few minutes to spare. Actually, it's the birthday present I made for you, but you left Vence a week too soon for me to give it to you.' She moved next to him and when he didn't take the gift, she ripped off the Christmas wrapping so he could see the framed photograph of the two of them on his motorbike.

In the picture, she sat behind him with her arms flung around his waist, their smiling faces pressed together.

Watching his reaction, she saw that Jean-Jacques remembered one of his friends snapping the photo. In the right-hand corner she'd written, 'To my love from your love' and the date.

'Do you remember that day? We'd just taken a glorious ride to Eze. Philippe said he'd never seen a couple so in love. He told us how envious he was.' Her voice throbbed.

Jean-Jacques took the picture from her hands and set it on the coffee table next to the eggnog. Then he turned to her. 'We had good times, Nicole. But all of that's in the past.' His black eyes glittered with a strange light. 'I should never have come here.'

She was trembling so hard, her legs would barely hold her up.

'Nobody forced you. Certainly your job wasn't on the line if you didn't. If my company is so repulsive to you, why did you bother?'

His chest heaved. 'Because I felt I owed you something for hurting you when I went away without a word of explanation.'

'What do you think you're doing to me now?' came her tortured whisper.

Jean-Jacques felt as though he and Nicole were back where they had been five years ago. Surely she still didn't have feelings for him. If she did, he was going to put a stop to any crazy fantasies she held. '*Mon Dieu*. It's happening again. No matter how many times I used to goad you, you always came back for more.'

Her eyes filled with tears.

'I was a cruel swine, wasn't I? Unfortunately it's a habit I can't seem to break.' He shot out his hands to grasp her upper arms. 'Is that what you want from me tonight? More of the same treatment?'

'Yes!' She cried her answer to his taunting question. It came from the very depths of her being. 'If it's the only part of you I can have, then yes — I'll take your cruelty.' Her hands reached inside his jacket and slid up that familiar hard chest to his broad shoulders. 'Please, Jean-Jacques,' she begged from every sensitised cell in her body, so on fire for him she covered his mouth with her own.

Nicole was taller than the average woman. In high heels, she didn't have too far to go in order to wrap her arms around his neck and prevent him from evading the full force of her desire.

It may have been five years, but what was happening right now felt as natural to her as breathing. One moment he was resisting her, the next instant everything changed and she found herself being kissed with a hunger she'd never even dreamed of.

Long, deep, sensual kisses that went on and on. He crushed her against him, melding her curves to his solid frame. Their hands roved frantically as if in disbelief that they were back in each other's arms.

His mouth stifled her moans of ecstasy, transporting her back to other flower-scented nights when they couldn't bear to be apart. It was like that now, and yet it was more. Much more. She knew she would die if she couldn't love Jean-Jacques like this for the rest of her life.

'Please, don't stop,' she begged when he unexpectedly wrenched his mouth from

hers, holding her at a distance while he struggled to recover from the passion they'd always aroused in each other on contact.

'Perhaps now you understand why I decided against telling you I was leaving Vence. I have no desire to hurt you, Nicole. Even if it was five years in coming, let's agree we've had our final goodbye.' He started for the door.

Ecstatic because he'd lost control in her arms, she followed him, considering what had happened between them, feeling a glimmer of hope. 'Whatever you say, Jean-Jacques. See you at the villa on Christmas Eve.'

* * *

The second he slid behind the wheel of his car, Jean-Jacques reached for his cell phone to call Nicole's brother. The same damn message resounded in his ear. Dominic wouldn't be available until the New Year. Letting loose with a couple of well-chosen epithets, he clicked off and shoved the key in the ignition.

He should have got out of Nicole's apartment before all hell had broken loose. The heavenly taste of her mouth still clung to his. His body throbbed with unassuaged longing.

One look at that photograph had unleashed every demon driving him. But it also reminded him his bike was still in the garage at the farm. Though he'd urged his father to sell it ages ago, the older man had insisted on keeping it for his son's return, assuring him it would stay in mint condition. Blessing his father's foresight, Jean-Jacques drove to his own apartment where he could change clothes first.

Tonight he needed the wind on his face and enough speed underneath him to find forgetfulness, if only for a little while...

And then he was going to contact Dominic and leave...before it was too late.

CHAPTER SEVEN

Nicole hovered near the tall French doors of the eighteenth-century drawing room, desolate because Jean-Jacques hadn't arrived. The Christmas programme was about ready to start. She was afraid he'd decided to stay away after what had transpired at her apartment. Her pulse raced to hear her mother's voice coming from the foyer.

'Jean-Jacques! How wonderful to see you after all these years! Please, come in.'

'*Merci*, Madame Giraud. The pleasure is all mine. *Joyeux Noel*.'

'What is this?'

'Nicole once told me you liked to collect *Père Noels*. I found this wood-carved version of Father Christmas in a little shop in town. I rather like the dark blue velvet of his elegant Capuchin hood and cloak.'

> ❄ **Tip:** When guests come to stay, place a small chocolate or treat on their pillow to make them feel more welcome!

He remembered! Moved beyond words by his unexpected kindness to her mother,

Nicole fought to get her emotions under control. When she heard her mother's cry of pure pleasure, she was lured out of her hiding place to join them.

Her mother caught sight of her. 'Darling, come and look at what Jean-Jacques brought us. Isn't this *Père Noel* exquisite?'

'He's wonderful,' Nicole said in a trembling voice. *You're wonderful*, her heart cried as her gaze sought Jean-Jacques's, but he refused to look at her. If they'd been alone, she would have forced him to acknowledge her.

'Thank you, *mon fils*.' Clearly thrilled, her mother raised up and kissed him on both cheeks. 'As you're our guest of honour this evening, would you be so kind as to hand the children their gifts after the programme? Their names are already on the packages.'

He nodded. 'Of course.'

'Nicole? While I put Father Christmas in his own special place on the mantel, why don't you show Jean-Jacques to his seat.'

* * *

With the greatest of reluctance his glance darted to Nicole. She looked like a heavenly angel in a stunning white wool suit with a jewelled Christmas tree pin attached to one of the lapels. Around her neck she'd tied a white chiffon scarf. She seemed part of the magic of the night. This was the first time he'd been inside the fabulous Giraud villa, which had been decorated to look like a holiday wonderland with decorated trees, swags of garlands and pots of fresh red flowers everywhere.

He felt as though he was in a dream and Nicole was this exquisite doll who'd come to life from beneath the huge Christmas tree with its coloured balls and pink and white lights.

Avoiding her eyes, he whispered, 'After you, Nicole.'

Following her voluptuous figure, he forced himself to smile and nod as they passed parents and staff seated on the Louis XV chairs and love seats. The group had assembled before a makeshift stage complete with a roofed stable, a wooden manger filled with straw, and a baby. Behind the manger stood several life-size cardboard cows and sheep. In the soft light, they looked real.

This was all Nicole's doing. Jean-Jacques was so proud of her he could hardly swallow for the lump in his throat. There was no other woman in existence like her. Debilitating pain shot through him because he was standing inside her world for the first time and had never felt so far removed from it.

As he took his place up in front, she gestured to the accompanist at the grand piano. Then the shepherds, followed by the three wise men in their homemade costumes, began to enter, singing, through the tall mirrored doors.

Next came Mary and Joseph, then the young narrator, who stumbled over his crook before taking his place at the microphone.

The parents started to whisper and chuckle as each child made his or her appearance and waved.

Hot tears stung Jean-Jacques's eyes because he couldn't remember a time when he hadn't wanted Nicole to be the mother of his children. It was never going to happen. Deep in agony, he didn't realise what was happening on stage until he heard Joseph cry out, 'I want to hold the baby Jesus, too!' Suddenly there was a tug of war between him and Mary, who was clutching the baby for all she was worth. The audience broke into laughter.

Nicole flashed Jean-Jacques a signal of distress. He bounded out of his seat and rushed up to the children. Kneeling behind them, he whispered, 'You can both hold him. Joseph, put your arm around Mary. That's right. Now just stay like that till the play is over.'

When Joseph finally did his bidding, Jean-Jacques released the breath he'd been holding and raised his head. Nicole's shimmering gaze fused with his, thanking him for saving the evening from disaster. Her loving expression was too much to handle.

Jean-Jacques couldn't wait any longer for Dominic to return his phone call. Tonight he would tender his resignation to Auguste Giraud. The older man was seated by the French doors. It would be a simple thing to seek him out.

By tomorrow morning Jean-Jacques planned to be long gone from the woman he loved…

* * *

While Jean-Jacques passed out the presents to the children, who were jumping up and down with excitement, Nicole worked with the maids to make certain the food and marzipan treats were ready in the dining room.

As soon as she could leave, she fixed a heaped plate for Jean-Jacques, then moved into the drawing room to find him. She had plans for them. Depending on the outcome, they'd never be out of each other's sight again.

But as she scanned the crowd, she couldn't see him anywhere. When she asked her mother, she said he'd gone to the library with Nicole's father. Uneasy because they'd disappeared during the festivities, she handed the plate to her mother and dashed out to the terrace. After walking the length of it past the music room, she stood outside her father's study at the other end of the villa.

She waited for several minutes but when it didn't seem that they would be leaving any time soon, she knocked on the door. 'Papa?' she asked before entering the room to discover her father alone at his desk. 'Where's Jean-Jacques?'

He sat back in the leather chair, eyeing her through shuttered lids. 'After we concluded our talk, he said he had an important engagement and left by the balcony stairs.'

'No!' She dashed back outside and leaned against the wrought iron railing to watch for movement in the sunken garden below. But she couldn't see or hear anything except the gentle rustle of the night breeze.

By now he could be anywhere and would

make certain she couldn't find him. Pain as real as if someone had repeatedly stabbed her left her immobilized. A deep sob welled up inside of her until she was convulsed.

'Nicolette. Tell me what's wrong.'

Her father was a cold man. It had been a long time since he'd reached out to comfort her. For once he'd caught her off guard.

She spun around, wiping the tears that dripped off her cheeks. 'Tonight was the company party. What was so important you had to bring him in here?'

'He said he had to talk to me in private. Dominic has been unavailable, so Jean-Jacques resigned to me.'

'Resigned...'

'Yes. He didn't give me a reason.'

'Dear God...I've got to find him!'

'Nicole — there's something you should know. Five years ago I offered Jean-Jacques a scholarship to go to Paris to study chemistry with the proviso that he work for the company after graduation.'

Shattered, she looked at her parent in horror. 'You paid him money to break us up? My own father?'

But it all made sense to her. Jean-Jacques had come home the new CEO of the company, a prize more coveted than the love of any woman. What man who'd expected to work in the flower fields all his life could have resisted such temptation? So why had he resigned?

'*Non, ma fille.* I was acting under your

brother's orders.'

She blinked. 'What are you talking about? Dominic doesn't have a treacherous bone in his body!'

'I agree,' he said quietly. 'Only once after the day he disowned me as his father did he ask a favour of me. Out of my love for him, I obliged without questioning it or his motives.'

Nicole couldn't take it all in. 'Dominic wanted my relationship with Jean-Jacques ended?'

'If you want answers, you'll have to ask your brother. For Dominic's sake, as well as my own selfish reasons, I'd rather your mother were kept in the dark. But before you're too hard on him, just remember that Jean-Jacques didn't have to take the offer.'

Nicole blinked back tears as she turned and ran the entire distance to her suite of rooms to phone Dominic. But with every step, her father's last words rang the death knell in her heart. *Just remember that Jean-Jacques didn't have to take the offe*r.

* * *

Jean-Jacques left the cathedral with his sister and her husband, bundling little Paul against his shoulder for the walk to their cars. During the midnight mass, the baby had fallen asleep on his shoulder.

While they made their way through the crowd, he was loath to give up his nephew's comforting warmth. Heaven knew he needed something to prevent him from thinking about what he was going to do now that he was no longer the CEO.

He was terrified that no matter where he went, no matter how many miles he put

between them, Nicole's memory would haunt him to the end of his life.

He felt a nudge in his ribs. 'What is it, Brigitte?'

'Don't look now but Nicole isn't far behind and is gaining on us with every footstep. Why don't you ask her to join the family for *réveillon*? Everyone loves her. You want her to come. Admit it.'

Jean-Jacques had known Nicole would attend mass with her family. But he hadn't expected her to search him out in this crowd. He should have known that leaving the villa without saying goodbye had been exactly the wrong thing to do.

'Leave it alone, Brigitte. There are things you don't understand. Tell Maman I'll catch up with all of you at the farm...'

CHAPTER EIGHT

Brigitte flashed her brother an accusing glance. 'Mark my words, Jean-Jacques, your stupid pride is going to be your ruination.'

Unable to abide her remarks because they were trampling over his bleeding wounds, he lifted Paul from his shoulder. By the time he had made the transfer to her arms, Nicole had reached them.

'*Joyeux Noel*, everyone. These presents are for your family.' She handed her packages to Claude, kissing him and Brigitte on both cheeks, then the baby.

When she lifted her head, she darted Jean-Jacques a glance devoid of emotion. Her eyes no longer reflected her usual joy. The drastic change in her demeanour, especially during this Christmas season, sent a chill through his body.

'If you two don't mind, I'd like to speak to Jean-Jacques for a few minutes. I promise I won't keep him long.'

'No problem. We'll see you later.' Brigitte shot Jean-Jacques a final fierce glint of disapproval before walking away with her husband and little Paul.

Once they'd gone, he turned to Nicole. 'I assume you came to mass with your parents. I'll run you to the villa in my car. It's behind the back of the cathedral.'

By tacit agreement they headed in that direction, forming part of the throng of people dispersing from the square. She said nothing and held herself apart from him. Even though this was the most holy of nights for locals and their families, there were still journalists hanging around for a chance sighting of her.

On cue the flashes started popping. A half-dozen video-cam artists followed their progress to the car, shouting at her to make a comment. With regal grace she ignored them as if they didn't exist. Still, it was a relief to get her inside and drive away.

He knew how much she hated the paparazzi. It was testimony of her determination to talk to him that she would face the media's scrutiny without Dominic or her parents nearby to offer protection.

I've always made you walk the gauntlet, haven't I, Nicole? But after tonight, no more.

One glance in the rear-view mirror told him the press hounds were in hot pursuit. But he knew they couldn't follow his car inside the gates of the Giraud estate.

Pressing his foot on the accelerator, he headed there with tyres squealing around the hairpin turns as they wound up the hill. Fortunately, Nicole had ridden on the back of his bike too many times to be nervous. In fact right now she seemed impervious to her surroundings. But he knew inside that beautiful skin of hers, tension had been building. She was ready to explode. So was he. The pain had to end.

The guard at the gate immediately recognised them and ushered him on through. Jean-Jacques drove beyond the fountain to the west end of the villa near a stand of dark cypress trees. It was the one place where they could have total privacy, yet Nicole would still be safe from him. Right now he was going to have to lie through his teeth.

He knew what she was going to say, so he decided to save her the trouble. Without looking at her, he said, 'After the way I left Vence, not to mention the way I've behaved since I've been back, I don't blame you for coming after me for an apology. No person deserves one more than you do, so I'll be blunt.

'As long as I lived in Vence, you were always a temptation, but not the sole meaning of my existence. After I moved to Paris, I discovered other women who had the same effect on me. When Dominic asked me to come back and head the company, I was flattered and thought it was what I wanted. But I was wrong. Paris has more distractions than I thought, so I've resigned from the company.'

'I know. My father told me.' To his shock he heard her door open. He jerked his head around in time to see her get out of the car. She leaned down so their eyes would meet.

Hers held a mixture of indescribable hurt and anger. 'I expected honesty from you tonight, but it's just not in you.' Her voice trembled. 'He told me about the scholarship.'

Jean-Jacques's worst nightmare had come true. Sickness welled up inside him.

'I don't blame you for taking what was offered. You now have what you never thought could be yours. Don't resign because of me. I'll never come near you again. But I have to tell you that if I'd known about this before you left Vence, I would have whispered, "Beware of Greeks bearing gifts". One day there may be a price to pay. I hope not. Adieu.'

* * *

'*Un moment!*' Jean-Jacques called out as he threw the last pair of socks in his suitcase. The knocking at the door continued. He'd refused to answer any phone calls. In frustration Brigitte must have told Claude to come over, hoping his brother-in-law could talk him into spending Christmas Day with them. But he wasn't fit for company, not even his own.

Damn Dominic to hell for flying to Paris and talking him into coming back home. Dominic knew how Jean-Jacques felt about Nicole. Dominic knew a lot more than he ever let on. That was what made him so remarkable. Until he'd allowed him to believe something that wasn't true, there probably wasn't a man other than his own father he admired more.

He still couldn't understand why Dominic hadn't asked him to take the position in New York. None of it made any sense. As for

Nicole, last night's devastating encounter outside the villa had written the end of their history. That one last withering adieu from her lips had said it all.

The knocking persisted. As long as it was Claude, Jean-Jacques didn't care if he hadn't shaved and was only wearing a pair of well-worn jeans. When he jerked the door open, his eyes narrowed in disbelief to see Nicole standing there in a two-piece suit the shade of hyacinths. She smelled like a garden of tea roses opened by the sun, and she looked so breathtaking, he thought he was hallucinating.

> **Tip:** Don't lose the fizz on your champagne! Pop a teaspoon (handle down) into the neck and enjoy the bubbles the next day…

He couldn't take any more. 'Unless it's a case of life or death, I don't know what would bring you to this door.'

'This is life and death. I just talked to Dominic. May I come in, please?'

There was an element in her voice and mien that convinced him she was serious. His heart did a violent kick. He stepped aside. As she moved past him into the mess he'd made of the living room with all his stuff still to be packed, he heard her breath catch. Her emotions had risen to the surface. Something traumatic had happened. He prayed it wasn't bad news. Nicole idolised her brother.

After closing the door, he leaned against it and folded his arms, not knowing what to expect, yet fearing the worst. She drew close to him. 'Jean-Jacques—'

He shook his head. 'What, Nicole? Tell me—' he cried softly in alarm.

To his shock, she got down on both knees and grasped his left hand. Looking up at him with her heart in her eyes, she said, 'I love you with all my mind, body and soul. I've loved you all my life. I don't remember a time when I didn't. This morning Dominic told me you loved me. He said that's why you went away.

'Now that you're back, would you do me the honour of marrying me? You're the man I want to be the father of my babies. You're the man I want to walk through the flowers with until the day we die. Please say yes.

'I already have a job, and so do you as CEO. I also have a home my dear grandfather willed to me. You've seen it. That lovely villa in Antibes, which is close enough to both our jobs. It's waiting for us. I also have this silver ring from Morocco my grandmother gave to him at their wedding. He told me to give it to my husband one day. It was meant for you, no one else. Will you let me put it on you? Please let me,' she implored him. 'Then promise me you'll never take it off.'

Jean-Jacques couldn't move, couldn't breathe. His vision blurred from tears he couldn't fight. When he felt the warm metal from her hand slide home on his ring finger, an enormous weight seemed to leave his body.

'Nicole...' he cried, joining her on the floor, pulling her on top of him. '*Mon amour.*'

He covered her feverish face with kisses. '*Je t'aime.*' He kissed her mouth. '*Je t'adore.*' He kissed her eyes and nose. 'I love you. Dear God, how I love you. I love you. I can't think what I've done to deserve you, but I've always wanted you for my wife. Yes, I'll marry you. I love you. I swear I'll love you to the day I die.'

She put a finger to his lips. 'Let's never talk about dying again, not when it's time to live. Really live.' She kissed his mouth hungrily. 'I want to get married as soon as we can. We'll tell the priest it's an emergency. If he gives us any trouble about not waiting for the banns, Dominic will fix it. He fixes everything. He was the mastermind behind that ghastly scholarship that took you away from me.' Her voice throbbed. 'But I forgive him because he brought you back to me.'

'On my way to Paris I figured he'd orchestrated everything,' he murmured against her throat where her scent was the sweetest. 'He knew when I hadn't proposed to you by the time I'd reached twenty-five, I wasn't after your money. He also heard I was leaving Vence to go to college in Lyon.'

She gasped. 'You never said a word to me.'

'I was afraid to, *mignonne*. Your power over me was too great. If you'd begged me not to leave, I probably wouldn't have. But without more education, I would never have worked up enough courage to ask Nicole Giraud, of all women, to marry me.

'Dominic understood me better than I did myself. When he heard through gossip about my plans, he devised a plan of his own to send me to Paris. I went with it because Paris was further away from home. I wouldn't be tempted to come back on weekends to be with you.'

'If only I'd known,' she moaned. 'I would have found a teaching job in Paris so we could be together all the time!'

'I wouldn't have let you, *mon amour*. My plan was to pay back your father every franc so I wouldn't be beholden to your family. By that time, if you were still free, I hoped to find a job elsewhere and ask you to marry me. Then I saw that photograph in the paper and thought you were getting married. My heart died that day, Nicole. It was the only reason I said yes when Dominic offered me the job. If I couldn't have you, I could at least come home to Vence.'

'Bless him for deceiving you.' She gave him another passionate kiss. 'He knew all along our wedding was going to happen. Do you know I'm marrying the most exciting Frenchman on the planet?'

'That is true, *chérie*,' he said very seriously, to provoke a response. She didn't disappoint him.

'You're horrible,' she teased, before they both chuckled. 'Swear to me you won't ever change. Always be my Jean-Jacques,' she begged before they lost all sense of time and place in each other's arms.

'I am a horrible man,' came his admission some time later, after he'd grudgingly released her mouth so she could breathe. 'I never let another guy get near you. I was too possessive. Those five years away were part penance for my sins.'

'The other part you'll have to pay by never

letting me out of your sight again. By the way, Dominic made me temporary CEO until you withdraw your resignation. Since I don't have it in writing yet, I'm ordering you to take a long honeymoon.'

Low laughter rumbled out of him as he reversed their positions. 'He's a man after my own heart. Where does my fetching bride-to-be want to go?' Looking down at her, he could drown in her gorgeous brown eyes.

'Anywhere you are. Merry Christmas, my darling.'

After a sharp intake of breath, he gathered her to him and clung. 'I think I'm too happy, Nicole.'

'You only think? That sounds like a true chemist talking,' she whispered into his neck. 'I guess this means we'll have to undergo hundreds of experiments to test your theory.'

Her mind was as exciting as her body, which was having too powerful an effect on him. He still couldn't believe his fantasy woman was going to be his wife! 'More like thousands and thousands. Come closer and we'll get started on our first one...' ■

GORGEOUS

We've all complained in the past that the Christmas season has become too commercialised — that it's all about where to go, what to wear and what to buy. So why not do something different this year, and show your friends and family that you care by **making your own gifts?** We all know that the presents we love to receive the most are the ones which our friends and loved ones have put thought and effort into. With this in mind, we have created two easy recipes so that you can make **delicious edible gifts** for your friends and family. We've even got some suggestions for the 'finishing touches' so you can be certain that your gifts will not only taste scrumptious but will also be **the best looking presents under the tree!**

HOME-MADE GIFTS!

Sugar and Spice

CHOCOLATE is a sweet treat on its own but paired with the spice of GINGER, it gives a new twist to the traditional. This year wrap up two Christmas favourites into one delicious gift.

Chocolate

- It is believed that cocoa trees were discovered in South America and from there the Mayan Indians brought them to Mexico. The Mayans used cocoa beans as currency and would create a frothy drink reserved for the upper class, made from roasted cocoa beans blended with red pepper, vanilla and water.

- Chocolate contains natural antioxidants, called flavonoids, which are believed to reduce the number of free radicals that contribute to medical problems, such as heart disease and cancer. Dark chocolate is a healthier choice than milk chocolate, which has more additives.

- We all know chocolate to be a sweet treat, but in Mexico it is also used in cooking. *Mole* is a sauce that traditionally contains chilli peppers, garlic, nuts, tomato, spices and chocolate.

- The melting point of cocoa butter is just below the human body temperature, which is why it literally melts in your mouth.

- Chocolate comes from a tree called Theobroma cacao, which in Greek means the food of the gods.

Ginger

- Ginger is the dried knobbly shaped root of a perennial herb that Chinese herbalists have relied on as medicine and flavouring for more than 2,500 years. The plant grows two to three feet tall and once the leaves of the plant die, the thick roots are dug up.

- Ginger is beneficial to good health, relieving everything from morning sickness to helping reduce cholesterol. It is commonly used to treat a number of ailments, including chronic bronchitis, menstrual pain, muscle spasms, depression, colic and diarrhoea.

- Ginger is often found in curries and is a main ingredient in many eastern cultures including Thai, Chinese and East Indian.

- In pubs small containers of ground ginger used to be left on the bar for people to sprinkle into their beer, hence the origins of ginger ale.

- Ginger is part of a beautiful plant, so in warm climates it is often used in landscaping around homes.

Chocolate and Ginger Gems

(also known as candied ginger)

16oz (454g) fresh ginger
20oz (565g) dark chocolate (pieces
or a bar chopped)
Sugar

- Peel ginger and slice into half inch pieces.
- Place in a saucepan, add water to pan, cover and cook on medium until tender, about 30 minutes.
- Drain, weigh and return to saucepan with an equal amount of sugar and 3 tablespoons water.
- Bring to boil, stirring regularly, until the ginger becomes transparent and the liquid is almost evaporated.
- Reduce heat and continue until ginger is almost dry. Toss the cooked ginger in sugar to coat.
- Dip ginger medallions halfway into chocolate leaving a portion of the ginger exposed.
- Let cool on a sheet of parchment paper.
Makes approximately 2 dozen.

Chocolate Ginger Shortbread

2oz (50g) dark chocolate, chopped
8oz (200g) butter, softened
4oz (100g) caster sugar
1 teaspoon vanilla
16oz (454g) plain flour
1 pinch of salt
8oz (200g) chopped crystallised ginger

- Preheat the oven to Gas Mark 2 (or 150°C). Melt chocolate over a saucepan of hot water, stirring occasionally.
- Remove from heat and let cool.
- Mix butter with sugar until fluffy.
- Stir in chocolate and vanilla. Add flour and salt; stir until blended.
- Mix in chopped crystallised ginger. Divide into 4 equal parts and chill until firm, approx 2 hours.
- Turn onto lightly floured work surface and roll out to 1/4 inch thickness.
- Cut with biscuit cutters and place on baking sheets with greaseproof paper.
- Bake for 30 minutes or until firm to the touch. Makes approximately 2 dozen.

Ways to wrap your home-made gifts

From posh prints to simple pleasures, deliver your special surprises in one of these unique and personal packages.

- Use **cloth napkins in Christmas colours** or cut Christmas material into 12" by 12" squares with pinking shears. Place your plastic-wrapped goodies in the centre of the square, then bring the corners up to meet and tie ribbon securely around the middle, creating a luscious pouch of magical medallions.

- In *The Sound of Music*, Julie Andrews sings lovingly about 'brown paper packages tied up with string'. Why not celebrate the simplicity of the **classic brown paper** package? Wrap **Chocolate and Ginger Gems** in plastic, then in brown paper either from a roll or a paper bag cut into a sheet. Tie with string and attach a name tag.

- Why not go the extra mile and make **personal name tags**? Be creative — write a line from your favourite Christmas carol, draw a Christmas scene or do anything that inspires the holiday spirit!

- If you're feeling the pressure, just buy small plastic sandwich bags with fun Christmas images on them. **Fill bags and tie a pretty bow** at the top for an excellent and easy way to show off your tasty treats.

- Remember, all of these ideas can be adapted throughout the year for **birthday**, **wedding** and **christening** gifts. Your gifts can be beautiful all year round.

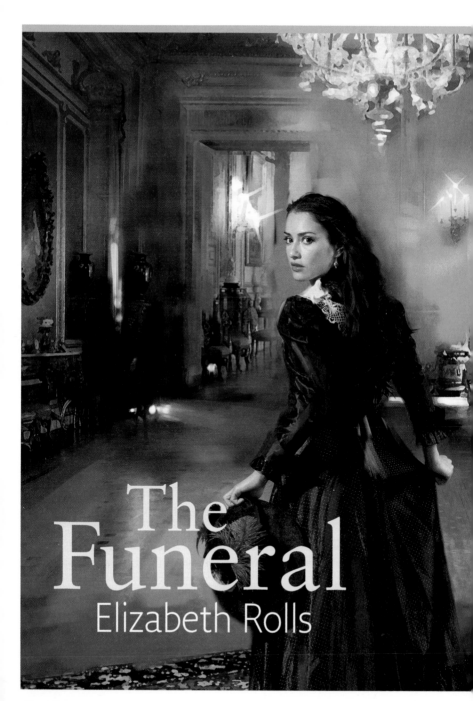

The Funeral

Elizabeth Rolls

Cornwall-1803

'No, thank you, Cousin Maria,' said Lucy softly, 'I really do not want any more tea.'

'Well, if you are quite sure, Lucy dear. I always find tea very helpful in trying circumstances. Perhaps a rest? You do look pale, but... the black gown, I dare say... Did you sleep well last night?'

'I am afraid not, Cousin,' said Lucy.

'No, of course not. The wind was dreadful, was it not? I declare, I scarce closed my eyes all night!'

Lucy bit her lip; she took leave to doubt that. Cousin Maria had insisted upon remaining with her the previous night and snored incessantly.

'Not that I grudge it, Lucy dear,' Cousin Maria assured her hurriedly, misinterpreting Lucy's expression. 'For I could not reconcile it with my conscience to leave you alone in your affliction! Not but what the chaise longue in your chamber is very comfortable, as I need not tell you!'

'No, Cousin. It... it is a lovely chaise longue.' She had her own fond memories of that chaise longue... *James, oh, James!*

'Yes, dear. So sad that you must leave all your pretty things behind. Such a tragedy. Poor, dear James. With all his sailing experience! Why, I could not believe it when the news came that he had drowned! Of course, dear, you know I am to remain with you? Dear William thinks that you will like to remove to the Dower House quite soon, and he suggests that I should remain with you there as your companion. So young as you are, you will require a companion!'

Lucy took a very careful breath. 'But, Cousin, would you not be happier here at the Hall? With William, Susan and the children?'

'Oh, no, dear!' Cousin Maria assured her. 'I must not be selfish! After all, I will be just as happy in a little house. And dear William is quite agreed that it should be so.'

'How... how very kind,' managed Lucy.

'Now, dear, you do not need to be grateful. I'm sure no one expects you to be alone at this time! You do look most dreadfully pale. Are you sure you are quite well?'

'I have the headache a little,' said Lucy. She had the headache a lot, but...

'Oh, my dear! You should have said! Nothing can make one feel more downpin. Perhaps tea after all. Shall I ring for a fresh pot? Or some pastilles to burn and laudanum!'

The fussing was like to drive her mad! She must speak out. Now.

'Cousin, if you would not be offended, I should like to be alone for a while.'

'Alone?' Miss Maria Stoker looked as though she had never heard of anything more appalling than a twenty-year-old widow of four weeks wishing to be alone. 'Oh, but dear William particularly charged me — '

'William,' said Lucy through clenched teeth, 'is not here.'

'No, dear. Of course not. He is at the memorial service with the other gentlemen,' said Maria, quite as though Lucy might have forgotten. 'And he told me most — '

'I wish to be alone,' said Lucy very firmly.

'But, dear, can I not comfort...'

'*No!*' Lucy almost shrieked. Instantly, seeing the look of profound shock on Cousin Maria's face, she controlled herself. 'I am sorry, Cousin, but I must ask you to leave me. Until the gentlemen return from... from the service.' Just a brief respite from the prevailing wisdom that poor, dear Lucy must not be left alone to dwell on her grief.

'Well, really! I am sure I hope that I have not forgot my place...'

'No, Cousin.' Lucy tried to smile. 'It is just... just that I should like some time alone to... to pray.' A lie if ever there was one. She wanted to scream at God.

Cousin Maria's face cleared. 'Oh, well, shall I read from the prayer book?'

'Alone!'

Finally alone, Lucy stared out the drawing-room windows. Rain and hail gusted against the glass. Beyond the weeping panes the gardens lay sodden. A tear slid down her cheek. A couple of miles away the sea would be crashing and boiling round the cliffs. This storm had sprung up unexpectedly yesterday evening. Like the one four weeks ago... It still felt unreal. She still woke in the night, reaching for him, only to find herself alone... last night had been the worst. With Maria snoring on the day bed she had not even had the release of tears in her unfamiliar bed. She had always slept in his. Whenever a door opened she expected him to walk in...She

found herself thinking, *I must tell him... James would laugh at that...* But James would never laugh with her again, or hold her in the night.

More tears slid down her face as she thought of the girl who had come here as a bride a year ago. She had loved riding out with James along the cliffs, loved the roar and fret of the ocean below, the cry of the gulls. She had gone sailing with him once, but she had been so dreadfully seasick that she had never gone again... at first she had wished that she had been with him and had died too, but she could not wish that now...

So hard to accept... even today, the day of his funeral; a funeral without a body, for the hungry sea had kept its prey, spitting back only the shattered yacht. Enough for her to abandon hope. Enough to bring William, James's older cousin and heir down to take charge. William, so different to James. So sure he knew what was best for everyone, herself included. Already he had slipped into the role, referring to his wife Susan as Lady Cambourne, and herself as the Dowager Lady Cambourne, giving his orders as though quite used to it. He had been rather miffed to discover that she had granted permission for any servant who wished, to attend the service... *Really, Cousin, quite unnecessary. The upper servants perhaps. Of course, I will rescind it for you...*

She had insisted. And William, plainly uneasy and no doubt expecting tears, had grudgingly acceded. Except, of course, for his own new valet, who had not known James anyway. All the staff here had been devastated when the news had come that the yacht had been found, destroying the fading hope that he might be safe. They had wept with her, down to the stable boys.

She blew her nose. James had been a trifle autocratic too, of course. Only when her father died, James had held her and comforted her; not told her bracingly to bear up, or looked away when she wept as though her grief was somehow embarrassing. He had understood her pain, despite the annoyance her father's constant gambling had caused him. He had pointed out that without her father's gambling debt to him, they might never have met.

And now William was here. William who had been so shocked at James's marriage. Doubtless James's will had shocked him further.

All he had said to her was, *A very generous settlement indeed, Cousin*. His lips thinly disapproving. She could hear the unspoken thought; *Generous indeed for a girl who brought nothing to the marriage beyond a pretty face and her father's gaming debts!*

And when she told him what she now suspected... what she so fervently hoped... carefully she laid her hand over her stomach. She had told no one. She still wasn't certain, but surely the nausea in the mornings and this aching exhaustion were more than just her grief.

Please, God! Oh, please!

Boy or a girl, she didn't care. Just a child. James's child to cast a little light through the grey years ahead. It would be easier if it were a girl without the responsibility of inheriting the Hall. William would be put out enough when she told him. If there was the slightest chance she was breeding then the estate would be in ward until it was certain one way or another.

She must tell him today. When the gentlemen returned from the memorial service. William intended bringing his entire family down from London next month.

He was going to be furious. Not that he would say so. That would be Bad Form. Like weeping.

Fact: In 1647, Christmas was made illegal. Festivities were banned by Oliver Cromwell, who considered feasting and revelry on what was supposed to be a holy day to be immoral!

There was a faint tap at the door.

She dashed away tears and blew her nose again. If Cousin Maria found her crying... 'Yes?'

* * *

Bartholemew Barnes was a gentleman's gentleman who knew his position to a nicety. Especially as recently appointed gentleman's gentleman to an earl. In the servants' hall his authority was unquestioned, although he doubted not that his late lordship's old servants resented him mightily as an upstart. No doubt his master would be making some changes!

No matter. He knew his place he did and it was not challenging desperate looking ruffians sneaking in at the side door! That was for a footman. The second footman at that.

He cleared his throat in what he considered to be a very authoritative fashion.

The intruder turned. And frowned.

'Who the devil are you?'

Barnes revised his thinking rapidly. Not one of the yokels sneaking in for a bit of onshore wrecking as it were, but a gentleman. Tall, dark-haired and powerful, although rather thin and tired-looking. One of the local bloods, no doubt, but what he was doing here dressed in rags...

'Where the hell is everyone? It's devilish quiet!'

Despite the fellow's positively piratical looks, Barnes found himself replying, 'At his lordship's funeral, sir. And who might...'

'*What?*'

Barnes permitted himself a ripple of sympathy. The poor fellow looked winded. Plainly he'd not heard the dreadful news.

'Which... which his lordship?'

'Ah, Lord Cambourne, sir. I'm his *new* lordship's man.'

The man blinked. 'William is here?'

Remembering that he was supposed to be throwing the fellow out, Barnes cleared his throat again. 'If I might know your — '

'Where's Lucy?'

Barnes stiffened. Much as he might concur with his master's expressed opinion that her ladyship's grief had led her into foolish leniency in permitting all the staff to attend the service, this familiarity was too much.

He drew himself up. 'Might I — '

Grey eyes blazed. 'Damn you! *Where's Lucy?*'

Barnes took an involuntary step back, but the intruder seemed to recollect himself. Barnes had the distinct impression of an iron will being ruthlessly self-imposed. 'No, wait. Look.' The man tugged a ring from his finger. 'Take this to her, please. It's important.'

Boggling at a gentleman who added *please*

to what he obviously considered an order, Barnes took the ring.

He did not like being followed up to the drawing room where her ladyship awaited the return of the funeral party, but the alternatives were limited. Something about the gentleman suggested that any opposition would be flattened. Literally. Barnes could have wept. This would cost him his job with an earl, this would!

At the drawing-room door, to Barnes's relief, the man held back. 'Give her the ring. She'll see me.'

* * *

Barnes felt more than a ripple of sympathy for poor young Lady Cambourne as he held out the ring to her. A lump thickened in his throat at her red-rimmed eyes and the tearstains on her cheeks. She looked as though she'd not slept a wink, so pale as she was in that black silk. Not a scrap of colour in her face, even her red curls extinguished under the black lace cap.

'Barnes — where did he — who gave you this?' She looked dizzy as she took the ring, staring at it... Barnes found himself roughly shouldered aside and, with a soft moan, Lady Cambourne crumpled into the arms of the stranger.

* * *

A deep voice spoke her name over and over. Reassuring her, telling her everything was all right, it had been a bad dream... just as it had every night for the past four weeks. And every time she had awoken to the reality of an empty bed... but this time, oh, she dared not believe... waking up hurt too much... just a little longer before she faced the truth... She pressed closer into the powerful arms before they must fade, already crying.

'Lucy! Sweetheart! Are you all right?' The arms tightened, warm lips caressed her brow, her cheeks. The ring was digging into her palm...

'Don't cry, darling. I'm safe! Look at me!'

Gentle teeth nipped at her ear, and she gasped, her body tingling.

'That's better. Open your eyes, love. And here — take this blasted thing off!' Swift, shaking fingers were under her chin, ripping at the cap strings and flinging it away.

She opened her eyes and he was still there. Thinner; dark shadows under the smiling grey eyes, but... 'How?' she whispered, lifting her disbelieving hand to his stubbled cheek. 'They found *The Albatross*...' A choked sob escaped her.

He kissed her tenderly. 'The stupidest thing: my rudder broke and I couldn't steer properly. A fishing boat picked me up while I was tossing around like a cork.' He grinned. 'Well, they *said* they were fishermen, but they looked more like smugglers to me. The problem was, they were Bretons and they wouldn't turn back in those seas anyway. So I ended up in Brittany with an inflammation of the lungs. Clannish lot. They managed to keep my presence very quiet, but obviously my message didn't get through to you! They brought me across last night.'

She shook her head, burrowing against him. 'No. When the yacht...' She shuddered. 'James, oh, James! Please, hold me!'

He obliged, finding her mouth and

kissing her...

A few moments later, Lucy was moved to say, 'James — what if someone comes in?'

'They can't. I locked the door when I shoved that fellow of William's out...'

An hour later the funeral party returned to be greeted with the news that the Dowager Lady Cambourne was locked in the drawing room with a strange man.

'She simply won't answer my knocking, Cousin!' wailed Miss Stoker, wringing her hands. 'I cannot imagine *what* Barnes was thinking!'

His lordship frowned direfully. 'I will deal with this, Cousin Maria. You ought not to have left her. And as for Barnes!' He strode up to the drawing room, followed by several agog local gentlemen, and his eyes widened at the soft laughter coming from within. He pounded on the door.

'Cousin! Cousin Lucy! Unlock this door immediately!'

After a moment's silence, a very familiar masculine voice answered; 'Go to the devil, William.'

His jaw sagged weakly, and a chuckle came from one of the gentlemen with him.

'Well, well, well. Seems James's death was slightly exaggerated. William, m'boy, do find his butler and tell him to chill the champagne!' ■

A Compromised Lady is Elizabeth Rolls's sparkling new Historical Romance — available from February 2008

The festive season is steeped in traditional fun — singing carols, decorating the tree, mince pies and turkey. Whilst traditions are important, we've got some *innovative culinary suggestions* to help inject some colour and spice into your usual Christmas fare.

A Yummy
Yuletide!

Swap the customary mulled wine for some jazzy punch with an original edge, which makes the perfect accompaniment to our **Cheese Bennes** recipe. And for a twist on the usual turkey, why not try a **spicy, colourful stuffing**, which is as simple as it is sophisticated. And if your Christmas parties are proving to be very enjoyable, there is even a **festive breakfast recipe** for those still having fun!

Easy Christmas Punch

BY MERLINE LOVELACE
MILLS & BOON INTRIGUE AUTHOR

Here's my favourite punch recipe!

Empty **2 trays of ice cubes** into a large punch bowl (for a festive touch, freeze cherries inside the cubes).
Add a **2 litre bottle of diet lemonade, 2 litres of orange juice** and **950ml of cranberry juice**. Spoon in **2lbs of raspberry sherbet**.
If desired, spike with **Cointreau and/or vodka** for an alcoholic treat!

Cheese Bennes

BY MARTA PERRY

8oz (220g) mature Cheddar cheese grated
4oz (100g) margarine or butter softened
¹/₄ teaspoon salt

Pinch of cayenne pepper
10oz (250g) flour
4oz (100g) toasted sesame seeds

Cream the first four ingredients together.
Add flour, sesame seeds and knead, forming into five long thin rolls. Wrap in wax paper and chill thoroughly.
Slice rolls into very thin rounds.
Bake at Gas Mark 4 (180°C) for 10-15 mins.
Store in an airtight container.

Breakfast Sausage Strata

BY CATHERINE MANN
MILLS & BOON INTRIGUE AUTHOR

Being a family constantly on the move, we rarely have the Christmas table filled with generations from both sides of the family.
Distant family members are present in holiday

celebrations through old family traditions — traditions like this family recipe we enjoy on Christmas morning.

16oz (400g) sausages
6 eggs
500ml milk
1 teaspoon salt
1 teaspoon dry mustard
3 slices of bread, cubed
8oz (220g) grated Cheddar cheese

- Fry the sausages, drain the grease from them and chop into cubes.
- Beat eggs and add milk, salt and mustard.
- Spread cubed bread all over the bottom of a 9"x 13" pan.
- Cover the bread with the sausage, then cheese.
- Pour the egg mixture over all.
- Refrigerate overnight.
- Bake in the morning at Gas Mark 4 (180°C) for 1 hour or until firm.

Cajun Seafood Stuffing

BY LEONARA WORTH

1 tin of water
2 tins chicken broth
1 tin cream of chicken soup
4oz (113g) butter
2 finely chopped onions
1 finely chopped green pepper
3 sticks finely chopped celery
Tabasco sauce
Cajun seasoning
16oz (400g) frozen prawns
16oz (400g) frozen crawfish
16oz (400g) sausage — hot and spicy is best!
1 small bag of herb stuffing mix
A few slices of stale white bread (break into chunks)
1 loaf of cornbread
2 eggs
250ml milk

- In a huge cooking pot, mix water, chicken broth, soup, butter, onions, peppers and celery.
- Cook until bubbling. Toss in a few drops of Tabasco. Add about a tablespoon or two of the Cajun seasoning.
- Turn heat to low and add shrimp and crawfish.

- Let this simmer while you cook the sausage separately, crumbling into little bits and browning it completely.
- Add the cooked sausage to the soup mix (you can drain the sausage if you want).
- Cook all until the prawns and crawfish are pink and heated through. Turn off the heat.
- Add herb stuffing mix and broken white bread.
- Then break up the cornbread and add that to the pot. Mixture should be mushy by now.
- Mix with a large spoon until everything is completely mixed and most of the liquid has been absorbed by the breads.
- Add the eggs, mixing well.
- Add the milk.
- Stir until the eggs and milk are mixed.
- Grease a large baking dish.
- Pour the stuffing into the baking dish and bake at Gas Mark 4 (180°C) for an hour or until it's brown and bubbly on top.
- Serve with turkey or chicken for a delicious alternative to chestnut stuffing!

Building Love
Shirley Jump

The cloud of dust kicked up by the Ford convertible zooming away could have choked a camel. Jessie Riley shook her head. Another of Tag's bad endings. If relationship failing had been a sport, Tag Lewis would have been voted Most Valuable Player.

He wasn't a bad guy, just bad with women. She'd worked for Tag's company for four years, the only woman on his construction crew. She'd become one of the boys *and* a sounding board for Tag's tales of lost love. Apparently he thought her mammary glands made her sympathetic to dating woes.

Tag stepped out of the cloud and towards Jessie. Her pulse reacted, as it always did to him. Tall. Dark brown hair, perpetual tan.

He knew how to carry a vest top and could swing a hammer with the precision of a politician giving a news conference.

'What is it with you?' Jessie toed at the tyre tracks. 'How many women have you broken up with lately?'

'Four.' He dusted off his Levi's. 'Since when do you keep a tally, Jessie?'

She hoisted up her toolbox. 'You're like a relationship wrecking ball. You should be condemned.'

'That's harsh.' He fell into step beside her.

'Look at this building. It's a disaster.' Jessie waved at the old hotel they were rehabbing. 'We've been breaking our backs trying to get it up to code. *If* we can do that, then we have to pretty it up. Even then, there's no guarantee you won't take a loss. It's a lot of work. And for what?'

> **Tip:** Never store white wine in the fridge, as it affects the flavour. Instead, pop it in the freezer for 30 minutes if you need it chilled quickly.

Tag stopped and put a hand on her shoulder. 'Close your eyes.'

'Are you nuts?'

'Close your eyes, Jessie,' he repeated.

She did as he said, trying to ignore the feel of his hand against her skin.

'Imagine this place in a few months. Do you see the restored front pillars? The glorious red carpet? The chandelier above, beckoning you inside?'

Crazy as it was, she saw his vision. She always could, which was why she'd stuck it out on his crew. 'You're a hopeless romantic.'

'I thought I was a condemned man.'

'Well, that, too.'

He let go of her shoulder, but hesitated when he looked at her. Something stirred in her gut. Something she refused to name. All she knew was that she couldn't hear one more of his dating tales. Couldn't hear about another pretty, fancy woman who'd turned out to be all wrong. And she couldn't look at Tag another day and see him smile at someone else. An idea came into Jessie's head. It was crazy, but if it worked... 'You know what you need? A rehab of your own. I bet I could — '

'Oh no, here it comes.'

'Make you over into a boyfriend any woman would kill to have,' she continued. 'Clean you up, get *your* chandelier shining.'

He grinned. 'And what exactly does that mean?'

'I'll give you better pick-up lines than, "Hey baby, wanna see my routers?"'

'I don't say that. Often.'

'That driveway can't take another break-up. Neither can the rhododendrons.'

'Those were Hilary's fault.'

'She took out her issues with you on the shrubbery.'

'Ok. I'll do it.' He considered her, and for the first time since Jessie had started working for Tag, she wished she wasn't wearing work boots, cut-off shorts and a T-shirt. 'But only because the landscaping is over budget.'

They began over a beer at Finnigan's that night, a favourite watering hole for the crew after a long day driving nails. She'd stopped at home and changed first, telling herself it was only because there wasn't any sense in trying to show Tag how to behave around a woman if she still looked like a man.

He let out a low whistle — along with half the crew — when Jessie walked into the bar wearing a red dress and heels. Her face went hot and something weird quivered in her gut. This was Tag, she reminded herself. Another one of the guys.

'First, don't whistle at a woman,' Jessie said. 'Not unless you're wearing orange and holding a road sign.'

He arched a brow. 'Then how do I show my appreciation?'

'Say something nice. And do it slow and sexy. Don't be in such an all-fired rush. Women aren't nail guns, you know.'

Tag considered this, then leaned in close. 'You look very different and... *amazing*.'

The heat in Finnigan's leapt twenty degrees. Faulty damned air-conditioner.

'How was that?'

'Uh... just fine.'

'Good.' He popped a beer nut into his mouth. 'Tell me more.'

'Don't go after your food like a caveman. Offer your date a taste first.'

He pushed the bowl her way. 'Beer nut?'

She laughed. 'Better. But that slow and easy thing still applies. What women want is *time*.'

He slid his watch across the table, grinning. 'Have a watch with your beer nuts?'

'Ha, ha. Very funny, Romeo.' Jessie sighed. 'You're hopeless.'

Tag slid off the stool, plucked up a beer nut, then closed in on Jessie. He placed it against her lips. 'Want a bite?'

Holy cow. What was she doing? 'Uh... sure.'

His brown eyes met hers. A heartbeat passed. Another. Then he placed his hands on either side of her seat. Jessie's pulse began to hammer faster than all the men on the crew put together. 'You know. I think I figured out my problem.'

She was having trouble breathing, never mind thinking. 'Really?'

'I'm not hanging my chandelier in the right house.'

'*What*?'

He tilted her chin to meet his. 'I keep looking at the wrong properties. The fancy ones. Their foundations are never good. What I really want is one that's not so worried about the cosmetics, about its façade. One with a good, solid base.'

'Are we talking hotels or — '

Fact: The first Christmas stamp was released in Canada in 1898.

'*Or.*' His lips were a breath away. 'I'm looking for an investment property. A long-term commitment. Know anyone available?'

'Well,' she said, taking a huge chance, '*this* address is vacant. But there's a problem.'

'What?'

'I hate chandeliers. Too much upkeep.'

He brushed his lips against hers. 'Good. Because I'm secretly a ceiling fan guy.' ∎

Shirley Jump has a fantastic new linked duet of books – **The Wedding Planners** – published in Mills & Boon Romance in April and June 2008.

Knitting for
My Life
Debbie Macomber

This morning, during a quiet moment at my shop, Margaret brought me a cup of tea. As I thanked her, I thought back to the early days of my new life — the life I have now. By 'early days' I mean three years ago, not very long in some ways but an eternity in others. Because that's when I began to change from Lydia Hoffman, cancer victim, to Lydia Hoffman, businesswoman, wife, stepmother, friend.

I'd been living in the darkness of fear and grief, and I emerged from it for two reasons. One is the fact that I learned to knit while undergoing chemotherapy. And the second is my father.

I'd started knitting a lovely cable knit sweater for him just before he died. I'd barely finished the first sleeve when he had the heart attack that killed him. He went so fast

it took us weeks to fully grasp that he'd never walk into the house again, carrying a new plant or a sack of oatmeal cookies from the neighborhood bakery. He'd never admire my mother's garden again, or sit in his favorite chair after dinner. Sorrow often comes most intensely in those small details, those ordinary memories.

My father and I had always been close, but we'd grown even more so after my two bouts with cancer. I survived; Dad didn't. It was my second diagnosis that killed him. I'm convinced of that and so was my sister, Margaret. I think she actually blamed me for Dad's death. It was almost as if Margaret believed I'd gotten sick on purpose!

My father was, of course, far too rational to feel this way. He encouraged me and comforted me and kept me focused on the future. And then he died...

Margaret stopped by one Sunday afternoon in the spring of 2003 — with her husband and without the girls, which was unusual. "Tell me what's going on," she demanded the minute she stepped inside.

Thankfully Mom was in the kitchen getting lunch on the table, so she couldn't hear the anger in my sister's voice.

"Good afternoon to you, too," I said, sitting down in my father's old armchair.

She ignored the sarcasm in my voice — and ignored my deliberate choice of Dad's chair.

Matt, my brother-in-law, looked decidedly uneasy. "How're you doing, Lydia?" he muttered.

I wasn't sure what to say. I was devastated, miserable, struggling, living one day at a time as I adjusted to life without my beloved father. "I'm okay," I finally said, leaving my grief unspoken.

Margaret stood there with her hands on her hips. "Answer my question," she said sharply.

"I don't recall you asking one," I said. I knew it was childish, but technically she *hadn't* asked a question. I reached for my needles and yarn and continued the pink hat I was making for Julia, my niece. Knitting has always had a calming effect on me and at the moment I needed that. My nerves were humming with irritation.

"Mom told me you're thinking of opening a yarn store."

"Oh, that," I said. "Yes, I'm considering it."

She frowned even harder and glared at

me. "That's the most ridiculous thing I've ever heard. You know absolutely *nothing* about running a business."

"True, but I know about knitting and yarn."

"Then start a knitting group."

"I plan to," I said, smiling up at her. "I thought that would be one of the most attractive features of my store."

Margaret didn't take kindly to my response. "And where do you intend to open this store?"

Despite every effort to hide my feelings, I sighed. "I don't know yet. As I said, I'm only considering it at this point."

"A business takes start-up capital."

"Yes, I know — " I wasn't allowed to finish.

"Just where are you going to get that kind of money?"

"Margaret . . . "

My sister silenced her husband with a single look. Matt rolled his eyes and cast me an apologetic smile. I smiled back, assuring him I understood. At one time, when we were girls, Margaret and I had a wonderful relationship but cancer destroyed that, the same way it damaged everything else in my life.

"A bank will never give you a loan," Margaret went on to say, her voice openly scornful.

A two-time cancer patient isn't a good financial risk. Fine, I already knew that. I had no intention of even applying for financial assistance from a bank.

"I've decided to cash in the stocks Grandma Wilson left us," I said, as unemotionally as I could. Margaret and Matt had used their inheritance for a down payment on their house. Dad had carefully invested mine and it had grown over the years, doubling in value. It wasn't a lot of money but it was enough for what I needed.

Margaret pinched her lips together. "That's downright stupid."

"Perhaps."

"What if you go under? Have you thought of that?"

I had, more than anyone realized. "It could happen," I agreed. "But that's the chance I'm willing to take. I'm going for broke. This shop is...an affirmation for me. I'd really hoped you'd support me in this."

My sister stared at me. "I don't think I can. You're putting your entire future at risk." She shook her head and sighed gustily. "But you seem to know that."

I nodded.

"Then all I can do is wish you the best."

Although the words were grudgingly said, I nodded again. "Thank you, Margaret."

I knew she'd be the first to say *I told you so* if my yarn store failed but fortunately she's never had that opportunity. In the past three years, A Good Yarn has given me everything I want — a sense of purpose, the satisfaction of doing work I love, new friends. And my own happiness has been a way to honor my father's memory.

But maybe most surprising of all, A Good Yarn has given me back my sister. ∎

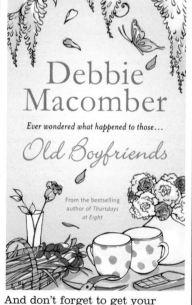

Baby Blocks

BY ANN NORLING

If Debbie Macomber's lovely story has inspired you, how about making this **beautiful baby shawl**? It would be a more-than-welcome gift for any new additions to the family!

FINISHED MEASUREMENTS:
33 X 45 INCHES (CRIB SIZE)

MATERIALS:
1300 YDS ANY BABY DK WOOL (600 GRAMS), 2 MARKERS

GAUGE:
5 STS = 1" ON #8 NEEDLE (OR SIZE THAT WILL GIVE YOU THE GAUGE)

NEEDLES:
26-36" CIRCULAR #8

GLOSSARY:
K = KNIT, P = PURL, REP = REPEAT, ST(S) = STITCH(ES)

STITCH NOTE:
WHEN YOU SEE *K3, P3* OR A SIMILAR STITCH GROUP, IT MEANS THAT YOU REPEAT WHATEVER IS ENCLOSED WITHIN THE ASTERISKS.

Cast on 171 sts

Border:

Row 1: *K3, P3* across row ending with K3
Row 2: *P3, K3* across row ending with P3
Row 3: Rep Row 1
Row 4: Rep Row 2
Row 5: *P3, K3* across row ending P3
Row 6: *K3, P3* across row ending with K3

Row 7: Rep Row 5
Row 8: Rep Row 6
Row 9–12: Rep Rows 1–4 once more

Body:

Row 13: P3, K3, P3, *K9, P9* across row to last 18 sts, place marker, K9, P3, K3, P3
Row 14: K3, P3, K3,* P9, K9* across row to last 18 sts, place marker, P9, K3, P3, K3
Row 15: Rep Row 13
Row 16: Rep Row 14
Row 17: K3, P3, K3, *K9, P9* across row to last 18 sts, slip marker, K9, K3, P3, K3
Row 18: P3, K3, P3, *P9, K9* across row to last 18 sts, slip marker, P9, P3, K3, P3
Row 19: Rep Row 17
Row 20: Rep Row 18
Row 21–24: Rep Rows 13-16
Row 25: K3, P3, K3, *P9, K9* across row to last 18 sts, slip marker, P9, K3, P3, K3

Row 26: P3, K3, P3, *K9, P9* across row to last 18 sts, slip marker, K9, P3, K3, P3
Row 27: Rep Row 25
Row 28: Rep Row 26
Row 29: P3, K3, P3, *P9, K9* across row to last 18 sts, slip marker, P9, P3, K3, P3
Row 30: K3, P3, K3, *K9, P9* across row to last 18 sts, slip marker, K9, K3, P3, K3
Row 31: Rep Row 29
Row 32: Rep Row 30
Rows 33–36: Rep Rows 25-28

Rep Rows 13-36 until piece measures approximately 42" and you have worked Row 36.

Border repeat:

Rep rows 1–12. Cast off loosely and finish off ends.

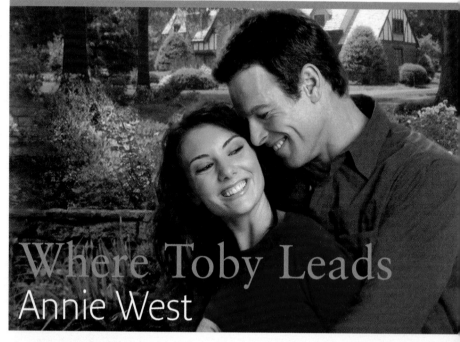

Where Toby Leads
Annie West

"Thanks again, Simon."

Jemma picked up her little dog and smiled at her neighbour. Laughter lines fanned out from his blue eyes as he grinned back. A stray lock of dark hair flopped across his forehead, making him look appealingly dishevelled.

"No problem. You know Toby's always welcome here."

He leaned forward and patted Toby's head. The Jack Russell Terrier squirmed and Jemma shifted her hold on him. Simon's hand fell but he didn't step away.

"Sure I can't convince you to share a coffee?" he asked.

His smile coaxed and Jemma almost abandoned her resolve and agreed to stay.

"Maybe another time. I really have to go."

He shrugged then held open his front gate for her, watching her walk the few yards to her own path. Then he waved a hand in salute and went back inside.

Inside her garden, Jemma put her dog down.

"Now, that's the last time, Toby. I don't know how you managed to get out and into Simon's yard again. But no more. Do you hear me?"

Toby tilted his head to one side, his bright eyes fixed on her face, his tail wagging. Then, abruptly losing interest, he turned and trotted off through the garden on business of his own.

Jemma shook her head. This was the third time in a week Toby had disappeared, only to

January

A new year, time for a fresh start! Begin the year as you mean to go on and take a moment for some post–Christmas relaxation. Get out and about and enjoy the crisp fresh air.

NEW YEAR'S RESOLUTIONS!

Make one, two or three—but make them realistic, things that you can achieve that will make you feel good about yourself. Start the diary you've always wanted to write, sign up for the course that's always interested you or make this the year you *do* lose that last half stone.

Take some time out for yourself

after the stress of the festive season. Treat yourself to a post-Christmas pampering session: run a luxurious bubble bath and relax while your favourite Mills & Boon romance whisks you away!

Buy your discounted tags & paper for Christmas! It means that next year you don't have to battle the Christmas crowds while carrying bulky rolls of paper — you'll definitely thank yourself in December.

Tip

Make your **marmalade** now as Seville oranges are in season. Don't forget to make an extra-large batch, because once friends and neighbours have tasted your gorgeous home-made preserve you'll always have people popping over for breakfast!

February 2008

01 Friday

New Mills & Boon books on sale today!

02 Saturday

03 Sunday

04 Monday

05 Tuesday

Shrove Tuesday

06 Wednesday

Ash Wednesday

07 Thursday

08 Friday

09 Saturday

10 Sunday

11 Monday

12 Tuesday

13 Wednesday

14 Thursday

St Valentine's Day

15 Friday

New Mills & Boon books on sale today!

16 Saturday

17 Sunday

18 Monday

19 Tuesday

20 Wednesday

21 Thursday

22 Friday

23 Saturday

24 Sunday

25 Monday

26 Tuesday

27 Wednesday

28 Thursday

29 Friday

February

gives you plenty of opportunities to show those you love that you care. And, as 2008 is a leap year, why not make this the month that you pop the question?!

On **St Valentine's Day** Danish men send a valentine known as a *gaekkebrev* (or 'joking letter'). This takes the form of a card with a poem, but the sender doesn't sign his name. Instead, he writes one dot for each letter in his name. If the lady who receives the card guesses the name of the sender, she is rewarded with an Easter egg later in the year!

In a **leap year**, women traditionally can propose on 29th February. According to legend, when St. Bridget complained to St. Patrick about women having to wait for so long for a man to propose, he said that women could ask men to marry *them* on this date, which comes once every four years.

How about an under-the-duvet day? Grab a DVD starring your favourite film star, be it George Clooney or Cary Grant, snuggle under the duvet and enjoy...

On Shrove Tuesday have a pancake party and experiment with the fillings — banana and chocolate, or ice cream and honey make a nice change from usual. Or try savoury pancakes — just fill with ham and cheese for a tasty treat.

March 2008

01 Saturday

02 Sunday

Mother's Day

03 Monday

04 Tuesday

05 Wednesday

06 Thursday

07 Friday

New Mills & Boon books on sale today!

08 Saturday

09 Sunday

10 Monday

11 Tuesday

12 Wednesday

13 Thursday

14 Friday

15 Saturday

16 Sunday

17 Monday

St Patrick's D

18 Tuesday

19 Wednesday

20 Thursday

21 Friday

New Mills & Boon books on sale tod
Good Frid

22 Saturday

23 Sunday

Easter Sund

24 Monday

Easter Mond

25 Tuesday

26 Wednesday

27 Thursday

28 Friday

29 Saturday

30 Sunday

31 Monday

March

s the month that we see the first welcome igns of spring, so use it as a motivator to get your rubber loves on and have a spring clean.

March is the month for the annual Spring Clean. This year turn this household chore into a fun workout! Turn your favourite music up loud, and banish the cobwebs while having a good sing-along.

It's **Easter** and kids love all the chocolatey treats, but make them work for it! Organise a proper Easter egg hunt in the garden or local park. If the kids are old enough, you could even make them answer questions before they get their loot!

St Patrick's Day
elebrate this jolly day ith a tasty pint of uinness in honour of reland's patron saint.

fact

Pubs in Ireland were closed on **St Patrick's Day**, a national religious holiday, as recently as the 1970s!

For **Mother's Day** this year, instead of sending an expensive bouquet that she'll have to throw away after a week or so, why not send a packet of seeds? The flowers will last far longer, and it will bring a smile to her face every time she catches a glimpse of them from the window.

April 2008

01 Tuesday

02 Wednesday

03 Thursday

04 Friday

05 Saturday

New Mills & Boon books on sale today!

06 Sunday

07 Monday

08 Tuesday

09 Wednesday

10 Thursday

11 Friday

12 Saturday

13 Sunday

14 Monday

15 Tuesday

16 Wednesday

17 Thursday

18 Friday

New Mills & Boon books on sale toda

19 Saturday

20 Sunday

21 Monday

22 Tuesday

23 Wednesday

St George's D

24 Thursday

25 Friday

26 Saturday

27 Sunday

28 Monday

29 Tuesday

30 Wednesday

April

is the month that we all start to come out of our winter hibernation! Make the most of the sunshine in the great outdoors.

fact

Did you know that **St George** is not just the patron saint of England, but also Canada, Catalonia, Ethiopia, Georgia, Greece, Montenegro and Serbia!

St George's Day on the 23rd of this month is a great time to celebrate all things English. So read some Shakespeare, enjoy some roast beef and a lovely cup of English breakfast tea!

fact

Did you know that the word '**April**' comes from the Latin word '*aperire*' which means 'to open', probably a reference to growing plants in spring.

NEW YEAR'S RESOLUTION UPDATE

- how are you doing?

Whatever you wanted to achieve, do keep going — it'll be worth it!

In France, an April Fool is called 'Un Poisson d'Avril', which means 'An April Fish'!

May 2008

01 Thursday

02 Friday

New Mills & Boon books on sale today!

03 Saturday

04 Sunday

Whit Sunday

05 Monday

May Day Bank Holiday

06 Tuesday

07 Wednesday

08 Thursday

09 Friday

10 Saturday

11 Sunday

12 Monday

13 Tuesday

14 Wednesday

15 Thursday

16 Friday

New Mills & Boon books on sale today!

17 Saturday

18 Sunday

19 Monday

20 Tuesday

21 Wednesday

22 Thursday

23 Friday

24 Saturday

25 Sunday

26 Monday

Spring Bank Holiday

27 Tuesday

28 Wednesday

29 Thursday

30 Friday

31 Saturday

May

This is the month when flowers and trees start to blossom and, as the crops grow, we see the summer begin.

fact

May Day is said to be a time of love and romance! Traditional customs include decorating houses before sunrise with flowers, and girls washing their faces in the dew of the early morning to make themselves beautiful in the hope of attracting a husband.

As **half-term** approaches, this is a great opportunity for the kids to help with the cooking — and to get them eating their five-a-day! Some great kid-friendly suggestions include home-made vegetarian pizzas, and making their own smoothies.

Plant a **herb garden** in time for the hot weather — fresh, tasty herbs can provide wonderful additions to light supper dishes and summer salads. So easy to care for, you will wonder how you ever cooked without them.

It's **getting hotter** and as the sun comes out so does your summer wardrobe, so start exfoliating and moisturising for shimmering summertime skin. For a real confidence boost, use a touch of fake tan to really start your summer in style!

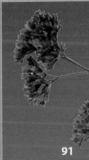

91

June 2008

01 Sunday

02 Monday

03 Tuesday

04 Wednesday

05 Thursday

06 Friday

07 Saturday
New Mills & Boon books on sale today!

08 Sunday

09 Monday

10 Tuesday

11 Wednesday

12 Thursday

13 Friday

14 Saturday

15 Sunday
Father'sDay

16 Monday

17 Tuesday

18 Wednesday

19 Thursday

20 Friday
New Mills & Boon books on sale today!

21 Saturday

22 Sunday

23 Monday

24 Tuesday

25 Wednesday

26 Thursday

27 Friday

28 Saturday

29 Sunday

30 Monday

June

The British summer really gets going... with Wimbledon, the Queen's official birthday, the Trooping of the Colour and Ascot!

June is the month of the **Wimbledon** fortnight. Cheer on Andy Murray and all our other British hopefuls with **strawberries** and champagne — just as they do at the All England Club!

fact

Did you know that June's flower is the **rose**, and that the ancient Greeks associated red roses with the blood of Aphrodite's beloved, Adonis? So fill your house with beautiful roses.

Father's Day: On 17th June we all get to show our dads just how much they mean to us. Get him a gift that he'll really appreciate, so if he's a golfer, how about a new golfing glove? Or just resolve to spend the day with him — it's probably the best gift of all!

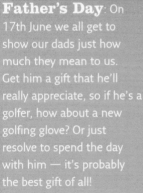

Celebrate the summer solstice with a get-together or barbecue with friends! Sit outside in your garden and make the most of the longest day of the year...

The **temperature's rising** so make sure that you never leave the house without putting on a suncream with at least SPF 15.

93

July 2008

01 Tuesday

02 Wednesday

03 Thursday

04 Friday

New Mills & Boon books on sale today!

05 Saturday

06 Sunday

07 Monday

08 Tuesday

09 Wednesday

10 Thursday

11 Friday

12 Saturday

13 Sunday

14 Monday

15 Tuesday

St Swithin's Day

16 Wednesday

17 Thursday

18 Friday

New Mills & Boon books on sale toda

19 Saturday

20 Sunday

21 Monday

22 Tuesday

23 Wednesday

24 Thursday

25 Friday

26 Saturday

27 Sunday

28 Monday

29 Tuesday

30 Wednesday

31 Thursday

July

Summer is here so take advantage of the hot weather to get outside and enjoy yourself...

If the weather is hot who wants to slave over a hot stove cooking? An enjoyable alternative is to organise a family **picnic** — after all, *everyone* loves a picnic. Even if the British weather lets you down, an 'inside picnic' will entertain the whole family!

Sweltering in the back garden? Try making ice lollies with pure fruit juice. Absolutely delicious, and guilt-free, they are a wonderful alternative to shop-bought versions—and are also great fun to make!

Many beautiful country houses have **open days** during the summer—check out the National Trust website for details of events local to you, and enjoy a day wandering through breathtakingly beautiful gardens, imagining you are a Mills & Boon heroine for a day!

With the Olympics next month, a great summer-holiday activity is to hold a '**sports day**' in your back garden. No need for hurdles, pole vault or other expensive equipment — kids will love competing in sack, egg and spoon, and wheelbarrow races.

August 2008

01 Friday

New Mills & Boon books on sale today!

02 Saturday

03 Sunday

04 Monday

05 Tuesday

06 Wednesday

07 Thursday

08 Friday

09 Saturday

10 Sunday

11 Monday

12 Tuesday

13 Wednesday

14 Thursday

15 Friday

New Mills & Boon books on sale today!

16 Saturday

17 Sunday

18 Monday

19 Tuesday

20 Wednesday

21 Thursday

22 Friday

23 Saturday

24 Sunday

25 Monday

Summer Bank Holiday

26 Tuesday

27 Wednesday

28 Thursday

29 Friday

30 Saturday

31 Sunday

August

is the traditional holiday month, both in the UK and in Europe, so even if you're not jetting off there are plenty of ways for you to enjoy this time of year.

From 8th August to 24th August, all eyes will be on Beijing for the **Games of the XXIX Olympiad**. During this time over 10,000 athletes from over 200 countries will compete in 28 different sports. It should be a wonderful 16 days!

fact

August is the month of **bank holidays**. But where did the term come from? It initially referred to days when the banks closed. Before 1834, banks observed a massive 33 bank holidays! These were mostly saints days and the typical church holidays like Christmas and Easter.

Enjoy the **summer evenings** and make time for yourself. Head out to the garden or a park with your favourite Mills & Boon book and relax...

Make sure you **take a break!** Even if you can't take a proper holiday, why not make the most of your local tourist attractions? Just take some time to relax and enjoy the sunshine.

September 2008

01 Monday

02 Tuesday

03 Wednesday

04 Thursday

05 Friday

New Mills & Boon books on sale today!

06 Saturday

07 Sunday

08 Monday

09 Tuesday

10 Wednesday

11 Thursday

12 Friday

13 Saturday

14 Sunday

15 Monday

16 Tuesday

17 Wednesday

18 Thursday

19 Friday

New Mills & Boon books on sale today!

20 Saturday

21 Sunday

22 Monday

23 Tuesday

24 Wednesday

25 Thursday

26 Friday

27 Saturday

28 Sunday

29 Monday

30 Tuesday

September

As the schools go back, turn your thoughts to making the most of the last of the summer—now is a great time to use up blackberries in preserves and pies!

Back to school— make the most of the warm weather and while the sun is still shining, walk with the kids to school. It's a great chance for fresh air and a bit of exercise, and a chance to enjoy the sunshine while you still can...

NEW YEAR'S RESOLUTION CHECK— how are you doing? Courses often follow the school year, so many will be starting now. Contact your local college for details.

Go on holiday! Travelling is significantly cheaper and you'll benefit from having missed the scorching temperatures of July and August. The weather will still be hot, but much more pleasant. Enjoy!

fact

Did you know that if you pick **blackberries** when the sun has been on them, ideally around midday, they will be sweeter than if you picked them first thing in the morning?

October 2008

01 Wednesday

02 Thursday

03 Friday

New Mills & Boon books on sale today!

04 Saturday

05 Sunday

06 Monday

07 Tuesday

08 Wednesday

09 Thursday

10 Friday

11 Saturday

12 Sunday

13 Monday

14 Tuesday

15 Wednesday

16 Thursday

17 Friday

New Mills & Boon books on sale today!

18 Saturday

19 Sunday

20 Monday

21 Tuesday

22 Wednesday

23 Thursday

24 Friday

25 Saturday

26 Sunday

27 Monday

28 Tuesday

29 Wednesday

30 Thursday

31 Friday

Hallowe'en

October

As autumn truly begins, the season of 'mists and mellow fruitfulness', get out into your garden to prepare for winter and make this Hallowe'en truly memorable!

This month is **Breast Cancer Awareness Month**. Breast Cancer Care uses this as an opportunity to make people aware of the ways in which it helps those affected by breast cancer. Get involved in events in your area, or get something going yourself, like a bake sale at work or a wine tasting for friends.

You can find details and ideas at www.breastcancercare.org.uk

This is the month to plant your daffodil bulbs. It's worth the effort now so that you can enjoy Wordsworth's 'host of golden daffodils' in the spring.

Time to celebrate all things spooky this month with Hallowe'en! As the kids will be at home for half-term, get them to create a Hallowe'en themed evening. They can make frightening ghost costumes with old sheets, and use black and red looped Christmas-style paper chains to decorate. And don't forget the apple bobbing!

fact

Trick or treating has its roots in the Middle Ages, when the practice of 'souling' was widespread. This was when poor people went from door to door, receiving food in return for prayers for the dead on All Souls' Day.

November 2008

01 Saturday

All Saints' Day

02 Sunday

All Souls' Day

03 Monday

04 Tuesday

05 Wednesday

Bonfire Night

06 Thursday

07 Friday

New Mills & Boon books on sale today!

08 Saturday

09 Sunday

Remembrence Sunday

10 Monday

11 Tuesday

Armistice Day

12 Wednesday

13 Thursday

14 Friday

15 Saturday

16 Sunday

17 Monday

18 Tuesday

19 Wednesday

20 Thursday

21 Friday

New Mills & Boon books on sale today!

22 Saturday

23 Sunday

24 Monday

25 Tuesday

26 Wednesday

27 Thursday

28 Friday

29 Saturday

30 Sunday

Advent Sunday

November

A month for bonfires, fireworks and keeping warm as the nights start to draw in...

Pumpkins — take advantage of the fact they'll be discounted after Hallowe'en, so you can buy them cheaply to make delicious **pumpkin soup**. So simple to make, warming on chilly winter evenings and utterly delicious.

Bonfire Night

Fireworks—do be careful. How about going to a locally-organised display where you can catch up with friends while watching the spectacular fireworks?

If you're planning on making your own Christmas cake, early November is the time to make it, giving it six weeks or more to mature.

fact

It used to be illegal not to celebrate the date of **Guy Fawkes**'s arrest in England! Hot food and drink including baked potatoes, hot soup, cocoa, gingerbread men and toffee apples have long been an essential ingredient of this usually cold night, and much is prepared on the bonfire itself.

fact

In Great Houses, traditionally, a dried bean was placed in one half of the **Christmas Cake** and a pea in the other. As the visitors arrived, they were given a piece of the cake, ladies from the left side, gentlemen from the right side. Whoever got the bean became King of the Revels for the night. The lady with the pea was his Queen for the evening.

December 2008

01 Monday

02 Tuesday

03 Wednesday

04 Thursday

05 Friday

New Mills & Boon books on sale today!

06 Saturday

07 Sunday

08 Monday

09 Tuesday

10 Wednesday

11 Thursday

12 Friday

13 Saturday

14 Sunday

15 Monday

16 Tuesday

17 Wednesday

18 Thursday

19 Friday

New Mills & Boon books on sale tod

20 Saturday

21 Sunday

Winter Solst

22 Monday

23 Tuesday

24 Wednesday

Christmas E

25 Thursday

Christmas D

26 Friday

Boxing D

27 Saturday

28 Sunday

29 Monday

30 Tuesday

31 Wednesday

New Year's E

December

It's Christmas time! In all the rush to make things perfect for that special day, don't forget to take time out for yourself and make your own list for Father Christmas.

fact

Have you hung your sprig of mistletoe yet? In medieval times, **mistletoe** symbolised purity and strength, and was believed to bring happiness, romance and peace. The tradition of kissing under the mistletoe developed because mistletoe was meant to cure a broken heart and soothe the differences between quarrelling lovers!

December can be such a busy month, but put time aside and pamper yourself this festive season. If you can't get to the salon, give yourself a deep-conditioning treatment at home, paint your nails and put on a face mask. You'll feel ready to face the world.

Go to a **carol concert** and get in the Christmas spirit. Your local church or community centre are the best places to go. It will also give you a chance to meet the neighbours that you rush past for the rest of the year.

On **New Year's Eve**, make sure that you have fun and feel proud of all your achievements in 2008!

Falling For Nick

Trish Morey

Lexi had less than ten minutes to live.

Hardly enough time for her brain to churn through the most pressing questions in world history.

How long would it take to fall?

Was it ever too late to make a will?

And what was sex *really* like?

She took a deep breath, trying to suppress the burn at the back of her throat. She wasn't ready to die.

'I don't want to die a virgin!'

Over the drone of the aircraft's engine Lexi could barely hear her own half sob, half declaration but somehow Nick seemed to sense her distress. He stopped talking to the other novice parachutist on his left and sidled closer. 'Say again?'

Lexi sucked in a breath as a strong hand squeezed her forearm reassuringly, the warm tingles his touch inspired making a mockery of the layers of clothing and thick jumpsuit separating his skin from her own. His perfect male face moved to within inches of hers as he strained to catch her words before they were sucked out the open door.

She looked into his intense, thickly lashed eyes and wished upon wish she could dive into those baby blues rather than into the void at her right. Same colour, very different destination.

'I...I can't do it.'

He untangled the gnarled, damp knot her hands had become and flattened them between his own, his body heat evaporating

any moisture. 'You're just nervous.'

Nervous! Here she was about to jump out of a plane, thousands of feet above the earth with nothing between her and certain death but a scrap of fabric and a few pieces of string, and he thought she was nervous.

Ha! She wasn't nervous.

She was pants-wetting petrified!

Even having Nick's warm hands cradling hers and the heady smell of adrenalin-charged testosterone assailing her senses was little compensation for knowing she was about to die. And she was much too young to die!

Hell! She was much too *inexperienced* to die.

For the first time ever Lexi felt her self-preservation instincts kicking in, overruling her lifelong quest to impress Nick Everett, the boy next door and the man she'd secretly been in love with for the past twenty years.

So far she'd bungee-jumped, white-water rafted, trekked up and down mountains and scaled life-threatening cliff faces simply to be with Nick, all the while pretending she'd loved every minute of it.

And she hadn't!

Lexi had hated every terrifying moment. Even her salt and pepper hair owed more to sheer terror than to her individual gene mix.

And all for what? Apart from those brief seconds when he'd thrown her a casual smile or slapped her companionably on the back when they'd made it to the top of a climb, she'd got absolutely nowhere.

She was still the girl next door. She would only ever be the girl next door.

'I don't want to jump!'

'Come on, Lexi. You're always such a good sport.'

Lexi pouted. Under that sporting exterior was a sex kitten interior just clawing to get out. Couldn't he see that?

'I won't do it.'

'Give me one good reason.'

'I'm scared.'

'There's nothing to be scared of.'

She gestured wildly out the open door.

'What about heights?'

'You won't be high for long.'

'Then I'm scared of falling.'

'Falling's the easy bit.'

'I'm scared of spiders.'

'Irrelevant.'

'I'm...pregnant!'

A flicker of shock clouded those perfect blue eyes. But only for a moment. Just as quickly the corners of his mouth turned up as he gave her shoulder a playful shove.

'Never. I know you better than that.'

Lexi slumped. It was the final blow. Not only did the love of her life not want her, he couldn't even bring himself to believe anyone else would either.

But, then, he was right, of course. How could Lexi Carrington-Smyth, eternal virgin, be pregnant? And the way things were

going, in less than ten minutes from now eternal virgin wouldn't merely be her lifestyle, it would also be her epitaph.

'I don't want to die a virgin.'

Lexi bit her lip too late — her confession was out.

Nick's eyes widened, his face creased with concern. 'You're serious, aren't you?'

She swallowed.

Ordinarily it would have been embarrassing but, given her life was about to come to an inglorious finale, Lexi figured there was no harm now in spilling the beans.

'I've thought about it...' *having sex with you* — *a lot* 'but I've never actually had sex ...not even once.'

He blinked once, very slowly. The gentle bump over his Adam's apple jerked up and down curiously. 'I mean, you're serious about not wanting to jump.'

Lexi grimaced and squeezed her eyes shut. Had she really just admitted her virginity to the man she'd most like to lose it to?

The pilot yelled, 'Over the drop zone.'

Her heart lurched and pumped crazily. Then again, she'd live the embarrassment down eventually — *live* being the operative word. Nothing short of engine failure was going to make her jump out of this plane.

'Ok,' Nick said. 'Next pass is jump run.

You still don't want to jump?'

Lexi's heart lightened. He wasn't going to make her! *May as well lay it on thick, just to be on the safe side.*

'I'm not jumping out of a perfectly serviceable aircraft. Not interested. Forget it. No way, José.'

He studied her shaking head for a second before shrugging his acceptance.

'Ok, then. You'll have to squeeze back and let the other jumper get past.'

She was already shuffling back when he continued. 'Shame, though. I was looking forward to that kiss.'

For a moment Lexi thought she'd misheard, but what else could he have said?

'What, um, did you say?'

He leaned over so close she could just about taste his warm, manly breath on her face. 'I always kiss my female students good luck before they jump.'

Lexi stared at those lips and thought about the many times she'd dreamed of being kissed by them. And she had a chance — now. If she didn't jump, she'd live but she may never get another chance to kiss Nick again. Would life be worth living on those terms?

And if she did kiss him, and the worst happened, maybe it was some consolation that one of her last actions on earth would have been pleasurable. For there was no doubt whatsoever it would be pleasurable.

Maybe she had been a trifle hasty. But she was going to have to act pretty cool if she wasn't to look a complete idiot.

She grabbed his sleeve so hard the Velcro fastener at his wrist ripped open.

'I'll do it!'

Nick adjusted his sleeve, and looked down at her uncertainly. 'You mean...?'

She nodded rapidly as she shuffled back into position. 'Yep! I was kidding. Sure had you fooled. Can't wait to jump. Let's get on with it.'

Finally his face broke into a broad smile. 'All right! Let's get cracking. This is jump run.'

> **Fact:** In 1834, Queen Victoria's husband, Prince Albert brought the first Christmas tree to Windsor Castle for the Royal family.

Nick attached the static line on the back of her chute to the clip in the plane so that when she jumped her parachute would be released automatically.

'Ok, all set? I'll ask you to climb out soon then I'll call a one-two-three-jump! Got that?'

'Got it.' Her insides churned, though whether it was from the anticipation of the jump or the kiss she couldn't tell.

'Then it's head back, arch and spread.'

'I know, I know. I'm ready.' *So kiss me!* She angled her face up towards his.

'And don't forget to count'

Lexi gave an exasperated sigh. 'Yes! One thousand, two thousand, three thousand,' she recited. 'Now, please, kiss me before I change my mind again.'

> ❄ **Fact:** The abbreviation 'Xmas' is derived from the Greek alphabet. X is letter Chi, which is the first letter of Christ's name in the Greek alphabet.

Nick laughed. 'Ok. Seeing as you asked so nicely.'

He dipped his head, placing a hand on her shoulder and slanting his mouth across hers. As their lips brushed her breath caught — there was no more need for air — the very touch of him filling her with sustenance. As if sampling her, his lips made feather-light passes until he drew slightly back. His beautiful blue eyes looked perplexed, his brow knitted in a frown.

Afraid it was over before it had begun, Lexi wound a hand behind his neck and reeled him in closer. She wasn't risking life and limb for one tiny peck!

But he was already coming back for more and the kiss intensified. Within an instant the pressure from his mouth had increased and hers opened willingly in response as his tongue explored, searching for hers.

The touch of his lips, the sensation of him in her mouth and his breath intermingling with hers — it was all so right, it was all so *Nick*. She tasted adventure and danger in a kiss that spoke of impossible hazards and untold perils and how she could conquer them all.

Deep within her a lifelong need found substance and grew, urging her body to open itself to him as her mouth had done moments before. His mouth left hers long enough to trail hot kisses down her throat.

Everything was easy after that. Just like Nick had said, her body arched, her head flung back and limbs spread wide as she gave herself up to the new experience.

Then she was free-falling, flying, totally out of control but beyond caring. The drone of the engine was drowned by the rush in her ears and adrenalin powered her being. Nothing else had ever made her feel this alive. Nothing else had ever felt so good.

Someone called her name. Was it over already? She couldn't even remember landing. Reluctantly she opened her eyes, surprised to meet Nick's quizzical scrutiny.

'So how did I do?'

'Not bad, for a beginner. But now it's jump time.'

Lexi's gut clenched as she looked around in panic. She was still in the plane!

'Brakes on!' yelled the pilot over his shoulder, signalling the all clear to climb outside.

Nick's hand wound its way comfortingly around hers. 'Hey, you can do this, you know.'

She swallowed, reassured more than anything that he didn't look too sorry about the kiss. She looked into his blue sky eyes and took heart. 'You really think?'

'I know,' he said, squeezing her hand. 'And I'll be on the ground just after you land to celebrate this first jump with. But that's not all. Maybe I've been missing things, but I'd say we have something else to celebrate after that kiss, wouldn't you?'

His blue eyes sparked with raw heat and fresh courage infused her veins, all her senses buzzing, every part of her alive. 'That is, if you want to, of course.'

Yes!

'Maybe,' she replied, trying to be cool despite the hammering in her heart, already angling herself steadily closer to the open door, impatient now to make this jump and take the quickest way down to the ground.

She'd braced her hands on either side of the door when he suddenly reached out from behind and pulled her shoulders around, pressing his lips to hers for one more brief, earth-shattering kiss. 'Maybe nothing!' he said. 'When we get down from here, you and I have got a serious date.' And then he kissed her once again for good measure.

She smiled as she climbed out and grabbed hold of the wing and then waited for Nick to give the word for her to launch herself into space. She smiled as she felt the jerk of the large dome of the parachute cracking open above her. And she smiled all the way down to terra firma.

Because nothing could scare her now. She had the taste of Nick on her lips and the hungry look in his eyes powering her blood. She could do anything!

And right now she was on her way down to be reunited with the man she loved. ∎

Read **Trish Morey's** stunning new Modern Romance **The Sheikh's Convenient Virgin** available from March 2008.

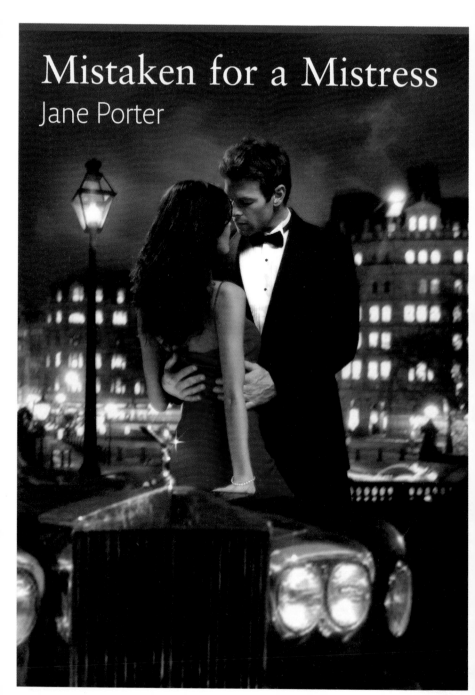

Mistaken for a Mistress

Jane Porter

'You'd like me to *what*?' Estrella's husky voice couldn't hide her shock.
This was the Gala Reception for the Marché International du Film, and the Marché, or Market, was the nuts and bolts side of the Cannes Film Festival. All the important people were here tonight.

'It could be a good time.'

Heat scalded her cheeks. Ignoring the financiers gathered around them, Estrella met the arrogant Italian's gaze. 'I'm afraid you've got the wrong woman.'

One of his eyebrows lifted. He seemed utterly oblivious of the others and the fact that this was a private reception, a very exclusive reception, for those with deep pockets and the right connections. The Market was the place where films were acquired, foreign rights were traded, and money changed hands. And the Market was the sole reason Estrella was in Cannes. 'You are Estrella Galván. Model?'

She felt as if he'd put a choke-hold on her. She could barely breathe. 'If you don't mind, I'm trying to do business here.'

His light eyes—a cool silver grey—narrowed. 'So am I.'

There was an embarrassed laugh and a low murmur of voices from the group of men. Some were amused, some uncomfortable, and Estrella's face burned from temple to chin.

'I think we could have a good time,' the Italian continued with the same appalling smile. 'Call me.'

She stiffened as he pressed a satin-finished business card into her hand, and immediately tried to return the card. 'I don't want it.'

'Why not? You look like a fun girl. I'm always interested in a party.'

Why was he doing this? What was he trying to achieve? She'd pulled a hundred strings to get an invite to the party tonight and she had just one chance — this chance — to interest these financiers in her film. The two-week festival was half over and so far she hadn't found anyone willing to back her project. The movie was everything right now. The children were depending on her.

'I appreciate your vote of confidence,' she said tightly, keeping her flawless smile in place, 'but Italian men don't really do it for me.'

It was as if she'd plucked the string of a violin. The air hummed, a note of tension zinging between them, and it was the most intensely physical sensation she'd known in years.

'No?' His voice mocked her.

'No.' She could feel him, feel him inhale, feel him breathe, feel him think. She trembled inwardly, shaken by the intense undercurrent.

'Yet your last lover was Italian.'

Her cheeks grew hotter. She shouldn't be surprised he knew about her love life. The paparazzi haunted her everywhere, especially when she'd dated Andre Mossimo, an Italian racing car driver, earlier in the year.

'*Last* being the operative word,' she answered with a smile, and yet her eyes blazed with anger.

'That's right. You dumped Andre after his tragic accident, didn't you?'

That seemed to do it for the group of international financiers. The executives began to drift away in twos and threes and Estrella felt pure panic. She was losing them! Losing out on her chance to pitch her film, and there was no way people would think she had a serious subject after the way this man had embarrassed her in front of everyone.

'Perfect,' the Italian said as they were left alone. 'Now it's just you and me.'

Estrella's eyes burned and she clenched her hands, crumpling the card he'd forced on her. She had a film without backing, an important documentary in need of distribution, and this man had just turned her into a joke.

'How could you do that?' she choked, overwhelmed by the opportunity lost. She'd pinned so many hopes on tonight. She'd needed tonight so badly.

He thrust his hands in the pockets of his black tuxedo trousers. 'Do what?'

But Carlo knew what he'd done and he knew exactly what he was doing. He'd heard Estrella, one of Milan's hottest models, had been angling for an invitation for the posh party, and curious, he'd been the one to get an invitation to her.

Having seen the beautiful Estrella in action before, he knew how devious she could be, and he wanted to know just what the calculating Argentine model was up to now. Why was she in Cannes? What was she wanting — or more correctly — who was her prey?

'Humiliate me like that,' she shot at him, tears filling her eyes.

He had to admit she was good. The tears looked genuine. If he hadn't known the anguish she'd put Andre through, he might have fallen for the shimmer of tears in her green-hazel eyes, but she, like his ex-girlfriend, Joy, was a top-notch manipulator. There was always something women like this wanted, and always someone new in the food chain.

'Come on,' he said, hailing a uniformed waiter and taking two champagne flutes from the silver tray. 'It's not so bad. The night's young. The festival has just begun.'

'It ends in a week,' she answered, refusing the champagne he held out to her.

'Seven whole days. With your looks, you'll have no problem finding your next cash cow.'

'Cash cow?'

Her voice had risen. She'd turned almost white. He shrugged and sipped his champagne. 'Sugar daddy, then.'

'Is that what you think I'm doing?'

'You are a beautiful woman.'

She flinched. 'And that makes me a *whore*?'

She sounded so shocked. Her injured tone reminded him of a Catholic schoolgirl. Carlo had to admire her skill. She was a far better actress than he'd expected. Or perhaps Joy had just made him more perceptive. 'Hardly, *cara*. You're exquisite. You carry yourself like a princess.'

'And let me guess. You have a thing for princesses.'

'Spoiled princesses,' he answered, tilting his glass, letting the bubbles rise. 'But you're going to tell me you're neither.'

'You think you know me.'

'Oh, I know enough.'

Estrella felt sick to her stomach. There were times she hated her career, hated that her face and body were familiar to strangers, but she'd chosen her career at eighteen. Modelling in Europe had been her ticket out of Argentina, and once she left Buenos Aires behind, she'd never looked back.

'You don't know me,' she said coolly. Her late father had been Count Tino. One of Argentina's wealthiest aristocrats, he had bought and sold small countries in a day. She knew all about arrogant, powerful men.

'Then educate me,' he said. 'I'm dying to learn.'

His bold scrutiny made her want to run and hide. He wasn't just sizing her up. He was projecting, picturing what she looked like beneath the glittering evening gown, and yet she was sure he already knew what she looked like. She'd been splashed over half of Italy last year in a very revealing lingerie ad. 'I don't like you.'

'And to think I went to all that trouble to get you an invitation to tonight's reception.'

Estrella felt as if she'd stepped in wet cement. '*You* sent the invitation?'

He sipped from his flute and yet his gaze never left her face. 'Yes.'

'Who are you?'

He smiled. 'I gave you my card.'

He had. She'd been clutching it, crumpling it into a ball in the damp creases of her hand. She smoothed the thick ivory card and glanced down. Just a name. And a phone number. Nothing else.

Then she read the name. Carlo Gabellini.

Estrella felt positively light-headed. It couldn't be. He wouldn't be…

'Something wrong, Miss Galván?'

She looked up at him, her mouth drying. He couldn't be Carlo Gabellini. Carlo Gabellini was head of the investment bank that was Andre's main sponsor. Carlo was the money behind Andre's car, and he'd easily poured a couple of million into Andre's account in the past year.

Carlo's head tilted and he smiled almost benevolently. 'Were you still Andre's mistress when you wiped out his bank account, or was that after his stroke?'

CHAPTER TWO

Estrella lightly rubbed her bare arms, trying to smooth away the goose bumps. Everything that could go wrong had. And now she'd been publicly humiliated by Italian venture capitalist Carlo Gabellini at one of the most prestigious parties in Cannes. 'I never touched Andre's bank account.'

'Then where did the money go?'

She shrugged impatiently. 'Drugs, probably. That's why he had a stroke.'

'So you left him.'

'It was mutual.' Why was she even having this conversation?

'That's not what Andre said.'

Estrella fought the rise of nausea. She felt positively sick. 'If you dislike me so much, Mr Gabellini, why go to the trouble to get me invited to the party tonight?'

'Curiosity.' His broad shoulders shifted. 'And prevention. I wanted to make sure you didn't take advantage of anyone here in Cannes. You did run a mean scam.'

'I don't scam people.' She was unable to tear her gaze from Carlo Gabellini's face. He had such strong bones in his face, clean distinct lines that were almost architectural. 'I'm here for the film festival.'

'The festival?'

'I'm representing a movie.'

He whistled softly. 'A movie. First a model. Now an actress. I didn't realise you had so many hidden talents.'

Estrella hated how he made her feel. She worked hard, and honestly, and she knew it. 'Like half the others here tonight, I'm pitching the project.'

His eyes never wavered from hers, even as he took another sip from his champagne. 'I knew you were looking for money.'

The insulting words he'd flung at her earlier, *cash cow* and *sugar daddy*, echoed in her ears but she suppressed her revulsion. She couldn't make a scene here. She needed the people here tonight. 'I'm looking for a buyer for the film — and if I can't find that, then I'll have to distribute it myself, but like everything in this business, that takes money.'

'Well, that's easy, then. You need money. I have money. Consider it done.'

She shivered as her beaded evening gown slid across her skin. Carlo Gabellini didn't respect her. In his eyes she was no better than sex-for-hire. And now he'd just offered her money. 'What do you want, Mr Gabellini?'

'Oh, that's easy.' His lips curved. His eyes narrowed as he smiled. 'I want you.'

She looked at him for a moment, unable to find the words for the intensity of her emotions. 'Me?'

He nodded once, his black hair gleaming in the light from the ornate crystal chandeliers parading down the ballroom ceiling. 'I want the same deal you made with Andre.'

For a moment Estrella heard nothing but a roar of outrage in her head, and then she clamped down on her temper, reminding herself of the hundred orphaned girls she'd met on her trip to India.

One hundred little girls without a future. One hundred little girls without a hope.

But the documentary could change everything. The documentary could give those girls a chance.

His gaze held hers. 'How much do you need?'

She lifted her chin. 'How much do you have?'

He suddenly laughed. 'So tell me about your film then. Do you play the starring role?'

'No.' And suddenly she knew that she couldn't —wouldn't—continue this conversation another moment. She didn't have to defend herself, and certainly didn't have to be insulted. She'd get the money, and find the backing for *One Heart*, without losing her self-respect.

Her gaze met his and she mustered a small, painful smile. 'Goodbye, Mr Gabellini.'

* * *

It was pouring outside the Majestic Hotel and Estrella did a double take as the slashing rain blurred the bright lights of Cannes.

She walked a couple of blocks in the rain before realising she should have waited for a taxi. She was completely soaked and freezing and she still had a number of blocks to go.

As she prepared to cross the street she saw a quick movement from the corner of her eye. Estrella felt the hair rise on the nape of her neck. Her sixth sense warned her to turn around. She did. She wasn't alone any more. Two men were behind her, literally right behind her, and Estrella knew that they wanted something.

She glanced right, left, looking for another pedestrian but the rain blurred the lights and the street was dark and Estrella knew she'd made a terrible mistake walking to her hotel alone.

Suddenly a dark Mercedes pulled up next to the kerb. The tinted window on the passenger side went down. Carlo Gabellini leaned across the empty passenger seat. 'Are you all right?'

Estrella shuddered and pulled her wet wrap closer to her chest. 'Good to see you, Carlo.'

His grey eyes narrowed. The car door opened. 'Get in.'

The moment she was seated, he accelerated, pulling away from the kerb. 'You're at the Carlton, aren't you?'

The Carlton Hotel was the place all the big American directors and producers stayed. 'Yes.' She was trembling so much it took her a couple of tries to get the seat belt buckled. 'Thank you.'

He shot her a quick glance. 'We should call the police.'

'And tell them what? That two men approached me on a street corner?'

'You could have been hurt.'

'I know.' She lifted her head and her gaze briefly met his. 'Thank you.'

Carlo's stomach tightened. Her eyes were beautiful. There was so much emotion there, so much intelligence and intensity. He'd seen the photographs of her, seen her on the catwalk plenty of times during the Milan shows, but her expression had always been hard and blank...empty. And he had assumed that she was as hard and empty on the inside.

But he was just beginning to realise that she might be far more interesting than he'd imagined. That she might not be quite the cold, vapid model Andre had described.

> **Tip:** Collect all your Christmas cards together and either recycle them, or keep them to make fun gift tags for next year!

Carlo had the Carlton Hotel's valet take the car and with his tuxedo jacket wrapped around Estrella's bare shoulders he escorted her through the crowded, elegant lobby.

She was still a bundle of nerves, but even jittery and wet, with her long hair slicked back from her face and his coat around her shoulders, heads turned.

Carlo felt the stares and heard the whispers as they passed through the lobby, and he was sure Estrella did, too, but she said nothing, her shoulders back, head high, walking as if she hadn't a care in the world.

117

At the lift she slid his tuxedo jacket off her shoulders and handed it back to him. 'I don't know quite what to say.' Her expression was wary. 'Tonight you destroyed me, and then saved me. Why?'

Good question, he thought, conscious of the small group standing behind them, one of them a popular American movie star. 'Fate,' he answered with a shrug.

Her jaw tightened. 'I don't believe in fate.'

The gold lift doors slid open and he put a hand on the doors to hold them for her. The group behind them was moving past, entering the lift, and Carlo stepped towards Estrella to let them pass.

As he stepped towards her he caught a whiff of her perfume, a very light floral scent that somehow suited her perfectly.

'Well, maybe you should,' he whispered into her ear. Then he lowered his head and kissed her.

CHAPTER THREE

Carlo kissed Estrella the way she'd always wanted to be kissed. His kiss felt absolutely right and he was absolutely wrong. And yet if she didn't think about him, just the sensation and the emotion, it was all so good, and it felt amazing. Exciting.

His hand slid from the back of her head down her spine to settle in the small of her back and the slow movement of his touch along her spine sent shivers of pleasure through every nerve in her body.

He touched her the way a man should touch a woman. He held her with confidence, the pressure of his lips neither hard nor soft but drawing from her a helpless, irresistible response.

This, she thought dizzily, was the first real kiss of her life.

A kiss that electrified, a kiss that could change one forever.

He lifted his head and ran his thumb across her warm, flushed cheek. 'See you tomorrow, *cara*.'

She tensed at the endearment. 'So what are you going to do? Tail me?'

He smiled faintly. 'You do have a nice tail.'

'I still don't like you, Mr Gabellini.'

'Good. I still don't want you to.'

Their eyes met and held and she saw a flicker in his eyes, a flicker of feeling that belied his words.

And then he turned around and walked away.

* * *

As Carlo headed back through the hotel lobby towards his waiting car, a voice hailed him from the bar. 'Carlo! Join me.'

It was Remi, an old friend from his university days who'd become a casting agent and had a hugely successful office in Paris. 'Wasn't that Estrella Galván?' Remi asked, signalling the bartender for two brandies.

Carlo sat down on a bar stool in the darkened interior. 'Yes,' he answered, thinking that there was something about Estrella Galván that had got under his skin. He liked her. He shouldn't like her. But he did.

'I thought you'd given up models,' Remi said, taking a bar stool opposite.

'I have.'

'So you're not together?'

'No.' Carlo was trying hard to forget the fire in Estrella's hazel eyes, the softness of her mouth, and the way she'd fitted against him. 'Why?'

'Because I'd quite like to take that woman to bed.'

He felt his temper flare even as his stomach twisted in knots. Ridiculous. Who was to say Estrella would even be interested in Remi?

Remi tapped out a cigarette and offered one to Carlo. 'Whatever happened to Joy?'

Carlo declined the cigarette. Remi had always been fascinated by Joy, an American model Carlo had dated years back, and a woman who'd used anyone and everyone to get ahead. Including Carlo's younger sister, Gabi. When Joy had dropped Carlo, Joy had also dropped Gabi, and his sister had been crushed. Gabi didn't understand what had happened to her 'best' friend.

'No idea.'

Remi flicked his lighter and lit his cigarette. 'I heard Estrella was trying to get backing for a movie,' he said, nodding towards the lifts. 'Unfortunately, she doesn't know the first thing about getting an independent film distributed.'

'She's not actually the producer, is she?'

'Well, it's not a big film. It's a documentary.' Remi blew out a stream of smoke. 'About India. And orphans. Originally she was only supposed to narrate but then the director—a young Irish woman—was killed just after filming ended so your model took over.'

Carlo's gut felt rock hard. He could see himself at the reception at the Majestic Hotel. He could hear his mocking words. 'So there is a real film?'

'*Oui. One Heart.*' Remi blew another stream of smoke. 'I'm surprised you didn't know. Everyone's been talking about the problems she's having getting support but no one's seen the damn thing and, hell, let's face it she's a model, not a brain surgeon. How intelligent can it be?'

Carlo left the hotel without having touched his brandy.

Was Estrella's film really legitimate? Was it a documentary about children, about *orphans*, and had he embarrassed her in front of the very people she needed most?

If so, he was the biggest jerk around.

* * *

After her hot shower, Estrella wrapped herself in a white hotel robe and opened the door of her room to her balcony. The rain had turned to a light mist and the night smelled cooler, sweeter, but it was hard for her to forget everything that had happened tonight.

It'd been a very difficult night and Estrella was tempted to throw on some clothes, jump on a plane, and head back to India where she was truly needed.

She wasn't needed—or even wanted— here. Carlo Gabellini had brought that truth home quite clearly.

In Cannes she was viewed as just another pretty but useless face. One of the reasons she'd left Buenos Aires six years ago had been to get away from an indulgent, self-absorbed mother and her wealthy family's indulgent, self-absorbed lifestyle.

Ever since she was little, Estrella had always wanted more. Not more things, but more emotion...more passion...more action. She'd thought modelling would be a ticket to living a more interesting life, but after six years of modelling she'd found herself even more limited.

Men loved the idea that she was pretty. They just didn't want her to open her mouth.

So she'd stopped talking. And before long she'd felt like a smiling doll even though on the inside she had been cold and alone.

Sighing a little, Estrella leaned against the door. She hadn't dated in nearly a year. Hadn't wanted to be with anyone after Andre, but Carlo's kiss tonight had stirred something inside her.

Carlo was nearly as unkind as Andre, but his kiss had been amazing. There was something in the way he'd touched her...something in his kiss that made her feel warm from the inside out.

How could a kiss be something that cleared one's head? Make one believe in possibilities and a life unseen?

A kiss couldn't.

It was just a trick of her mind, a play of the imagination. She was tired. She was overwhelmed. Time to go to bed. Tomorrow was the screening of *One Heart* and her most important day in Cannes yet.

The screening was everything. The screening would convey the huge need, telling in colour and pictures what words couldn't

say. People would see the village orphanage, the dozens of small girls who'd been abandoned by their families, and the fate of older girls who were sold into prostitution.

Estrella turned out the light knowing that in the morning everything her friend Allie had worked for could finally come true.

* * *

The ringing of the phone woke Estrella.

'I hate to be the bearer of bad news, but you'd better come downstairs.'

The husky male voice belonged to only one man. 'I'm not interested,' she answered, annoyed that she'd recognised Carlo Gabellini's voice in the first place.

'You will be.'

Estrella sat up in bed. 'I don't have time for this.'

'I think you do.' His voice gentled. 'Estrella, you better come down. It's important.'

Something in his tone sent shivers up and down her spine. He sounded worried. Very worried. But Carlo wasn't her friend and he wasn't on her side so why should he be worried for her? 'You're scaring me.'

'I'm sorry.' There was a moment's hesitation before he spoke again. 'Your screening's been cancelled.'

CHAPTER FOUR

They'd cancelled her screening?

Estrella felt as if someone had dumped a bucket of ice water over her head. The screening couldn't have been cancelled. It was her best chance for interesting a major distributor. 'It can't be. I've been placing ads.

Handing out flyers.'

'Apparently there's been some kind of mix-up. It seems the theatre—'

Carlo never had the chance to finish. She hung up on him and dived out of bed and into clothes.

Estrella reached the lobby in less than three minutes. She was still roping her hair into a long dark ponytail when the lift doors slid open. Carlo was in the lobby, waiting.

'What's going on?' she demanded, tucking the hem of her green gauze blouse into her faded jeans.

He handed her an espresso to go. 'Come on. I've a car waiting. We'll head over to the festival office together.'

But in the back of his limousine Estrella could barely hold her cup of coffee, her hand shook so badly. 'I don't understand.'

'I wanted more information.'

'Why?'

'I was curious about your project.'

'Because you didn't think there really was a project, did you?'

'You're a model, Estrella.'

'Go to hell!' She leaned forward to rap on the glass partition between the back seat and the driver. 'Please pull over. I want to get out.'

Carlo put his hand on her forearm. 'Don't be silly. We're almost there.'

She shook him off. 'I don't care. I don't need you judging me. My life is hard enough without you making it tougher.'

The driver parked at the kerb. Estrella quickly gathered her purse and binder filled with project information including script, bios, and film objective.

Carlo swore beneath his breath. 'I'm trying to help you, Estrella.'

'Help me?' she retorted, gripping the car door handle. 'Just like you helped me last night at the Majestic?' He was incredible. He really was. 'Well, stop helping me because your idea of help is killing my film.'

Estrella slid out of the back of Carlo's car and dashed to the Festival International du Film's office. But her breathless request for help was met with near indifference.

'The theatre is no longer available,' the woman in the festival's front office replied as she rifled through a stack of forms.

Estrella set her heavy binder down on the counter. 'But how? Why?'

'The screening room in the Riviera was double-booked. One film had to be bumped. Yours.'

'Yes, but we've been booked into that space for weeks.' Estrella rummaged in her bag for her own paperwork. 'I have a confirmation here—'

'It's just a piece of paper. Everybody has paper. Everybody has a film. This is Cannes.'

Estrella's fingers curled around her confirmation slip. She felt as if a shard of ice had lodged itself in her chest. 'There must be something you can do.'

'It's out of my hands.'

Estrella didn't believe it. 'When was the decision made to bump my documentary?'

The woman muttered something in French and moved to her computer to open a file.

'Late last night.' She looked up at Estrella. 'There was a meeting after the grand reception at the Majestic.'

The reception at the Majestic. That was the event she'd attended last night. Her movie had been bumped after the reception...her movie had been bumped after Carlo had discredited her in front of everyone.

It was hopeless. And she was exhausted. Everything was so damn hard and she'd been fighting for this project so long.

Wordlessly Estrella left the festival office, her shoulders slumped with fatigue. She stepped out into the sunshine, blinked against the brightness of the light, and saw Carlo Gabellini standing at the kerb next to his car waiting for her.

> **Tip:** Awkward shaped parcel? Collect boxes throughout the year for just such an occasion!

She snapped. Her control, her patience, her perspective—all were long gone, and she marched on him wanting blood. 'You did this,' she cried. 'This is *your* fault. The screening was cancelled after you turned me into a stupid joke!'

'Wait!' He held his hands up. 'Slow down.'

'Slow down? Like hell! I came here to get a film distributed, and you've blown it to bits. You've blown my reputation, too. How do you live with yourself, Gabellini? How can you step on people this way?'

'I haven't—'

'You *have*.' Her heart was pounding. Her hands were shaking. None of this would have

happened if he'd just minded his own business. 'You know every theatre has been booked for months, some since the end of last year's festival. There's no way we're going to get another space at the last minute.'

His brow creased. 'I'm sorry.'

Tears burned her eyes and yet she'd rather burn in hell than let them fall. 'No, you're not. You did exactly what you set out to do. You've totally discredited me as a legitimate filmmaker.' She clenched her binder against her chest. 'But you know, Carlo, you didn't hurt me. You hurt dozens of little girls.'

She flipped open the binder and pointed to a page of black-and-white photographs. 'These babies were all supposed to be put to death at birth. Why? They're girls. In some villages in Tamil Nadu they still kill female children at birth. It's believed that the birth of a female child is a curse to the family.'

She lifted her head and looked at him, pain and outrage shimmering in her eyes. '*One Heart* is the story of an orphanage in Tamil Nadu trying to save these unwanted babies. *One Heart* is about poor people in southern India trying to make a difference despite their poverty.'

She ripped the page of photographs from the binder and thrust it at him. 'It's a film that should have been seen, and it would have been, if it weren't for you.'

Carlo gazed down at the page of photographs. There were a half-dozen photos and all the girls were very young, mostly toddlers between one and three. They had beautiful brown eyes and sombre expressions. 'I didn't cancel your screening,' he said quietly.

'I wouldn't do that to you.'

'But you did embarrass me.'

He couldn't remember when he'd last felt so small, mean and petty. She was right. He had embarrassed her. He'd thought she was using people, thought she was playing them—working a new angle just like Joy had worked him. And just like Andre had said Estrella had worked him.

But Andre lied.

Estrella wasn't like Joy. Estrella had never been callous and self-absorbed.

'Why?' Estrella demanded huskily.

He swallowed hard, weighed down by guilt. 'I thought I was protecting the others.' God, the words sounded thin, the excuse flimsy. 'You were with Andre when he had money, but then after his accident and after he lost everything you disappeared on him.'

Estrella shook her head, her lips quivering with hurt and disgust. 'Not that you're interested in facts, but I didn't use Andre. He used me. He emptied my bank account. He slept with other women behind my back. And when he had that stroke, he wasn't alone. He was in bed, naked, snorting a funny white powder with one of my best friends.'

Carlo felt as if she'd hit him with a hammer. 'I don't know what to say.'

'Of course not. It's easier to be cruel, isn't it?'

CHAPTER FIVE

Estrella had told Carlo to stay away from her, and he had.

Then she allowed herself a couple hours to feel sorry for herself before she gave herself a major attitude adjustment.

She was not going to let this film go unnoticed. If she couldn't get a screening, then she'd interest distributors another way. She'd paper Cannes with a synopsis of *One Heart*. She'd run a thousand copies and leave them everywhere.

It sounded like a good plan until she actually had to distribute a thousand flyers. Late the next morning Estrella stood at the edge of the Croisette, the street lined with huge tents with names like the American Pavilion and the British Pavilion, each tent packed with people drinking, schmoozing and making deals, and tried to forget that her feet ached and her arms were sore.

Aches and pains didn't matter. The girls mattered. Allie's dream mattered. Important stuff mattered. Not blistered heels and tender arms.

Remembering the girls motivated Estrella. She was passing the Italian Pavilion when a voice hailed her from inside. 'How is it going?'

She tensed. Not him again. There were thousands of people in Cannes and she had to run into Carlo Gabellini every five minutes.

Estrella clutched the thick stack of flyers and studied him as he wandered to the edge of the Italian Pavilion.

He looked extraordinary this afternoon. White shirt casually unbuttoned at the throat. Light grey trousers in a fine Italian fabric. Beautiful leather belt and shoes. And, of course, that amazing face of his.

'It's going fine,' she answered, knowing she was on the brink of collapse but unwilling to tell him that.

'Why don't you come in, rest a bit, have a cold drink?'

'I can't. I've still a couple of hundred flyers to hand out.'

'Can I have one?'

Wordlessly she handed him one and he studied the paper. 'It's a project overview,' she said.

'Good job,' he said, skimming the information. 'You've got it all here. Outline of the project, bios, script synopsis, contact information. Well done.' He looked up at her, nodding with approval. 'I haven't seen such a polished, comprehensive project overview here.'

She didn't know if it was the expression in his eyes or his words of approval, but she flushed with pleasure. It was so nice to hear something positive, but the moment she realised how much his compliment mattered to her, she blasted herself for being a fool.

Carlo Gabellini's opinion wasn't important. He was the bad guy. He'd made her trip to Cannes an absolute nightmare.

'Here, give me half the stack,' he added. 'I'll help you pass them out. That way you won't be on your feet all day.'

Was this his way of saying sorry? She wasn't sure if she should even accept his apology, if he made one.

'I'm good at this sort of thing,' he added seriously. 'I used to work in a stock exchange. I ran paper all over the building. I was very fast. Very reliable.'

Estrella's lips twitched. Even if she wanted to refuse his offer, she couldn't. She needed his help too badly. The children needed his help too badly. 'I've already covered the area from the Carlton to the Grand Hotel. I've the rest of the Croisette to go.'

'Fine.' His silver gaze met hers and held for a moment, and then another moment longer. Estrella felt a cool shiver of sensation race through her. 'I'll take the right side of the promenade. You take the left. We'll meet at the end.'

It was nearly two hours before she finished working her side of the Croisette. Fans had begun to recognise her and she'd spent almost as much time signing autographs and posing for pictures as she had handing out flyers.

'How about that cold drink now?' Carlo said, stepping through the crowd and rescuing Estrella from yet another photo session.

She nodded gratefully. She felt parched and her head throbbed from the bright light and noise of the crowd. 'Please.'

His brow furrowed and he lightly pressed the back of his hand to her forehead. 'Are you all right, *cara?*'

His hand felt wonderful, cool and firm, and she managed a small smile. 'Just thirsty.'

He nodded but his expression remained watchful. 'Let's get you in the shade,' he said, placing a protective hand in the middle of her back, steering her away from the packed promenade towards the steps of the distinguished Martinez Hotel.

She suppressed a shiver as his fingers pressed against her back. She loved the way he touched her, loved his confidence and his ease in crowds. He moved them through the hotel lobby to the terrace restaurant, where they were seated at a window table, with the tall windows wide-open to capture the afternoon breeze.

Carlo ordered the afternoon tea for them and as they sat at the small table with the crisp white linen cloth Estrella began to relax. The sun was glorious. From their table they could see the crowded beach with neat rows of striped umbrellas and a sea of bronzed bodies.

'I didn't know Andre had a drug problem.' Carlo's voice broke the quiet.

'It was a big problem,' she answered quietly. 'But he worked hard to hide it from you.'

'Is that where all the money went?'

Her shoulders shifted. She didn't like talking about Andre. Didn't like thinking about him. Andre had been an extremely hurtful person. Dating him had been one of the lowest points in her life. 'That and gambling. He got in deep with some of the wrong people, but I don't know the details. He didn't discuss things like that with me.'

Carlo sighed and ran a hand through his dark crisp hair, ruffling it thoroughly. 'Wow. I read it all wrong. I put two and two together and got seven. I'm sorry.'

She looked up at him and her heart did a little jump. It was so silly. There was no way she could allow herself to get involved with Carlo, and yet there was something about him that she responded to.

'You weren't the only one that trusted Andre,' she said after a moment, trying to ignore the lurch inside of her, that little part of her that hoped. Maybe one day she would be taken seriously. Maybe one day she'd find the right man, and real love. 'Lots of people did. He could be charming when he wanted to be. He knew how to play it.' She took a deep breath. 'He certainly played me.'

'I'm sorry he hurt you.'

She shrugged. 'If he hadn't, I wouldn't have wanted to escape Europe for a while, and I wouldn't have agreed to narrate the film. I guess you can say that Andre's betrayal led me to finding my mission.'

Carlo's intense gaze met hers. 'Fate.'

'No.'

'Fate,' he repeated.

And the silence stretched between them, a long taut silence that somehow wrapped them together.

Fate.

Estrella drew a shallow breath, her pulse quickened, and she suddenly wondered if perhaps he was right. Perhaps fate had also brought her and Carlo together. Perhaps there was something greater ahead for both of them...a destiny together.

No.

Absolutely not. Estrella lifted a hand as if to break the spell. It was the heat. The lingering effects of the sun. It was her fatigue.

It wasn't Carlo and it wasn't fate and she

couldn't let herself enjoy his company this much. He was impossible. He'd made her life utterly miserable and there was no way she'd let him connect with her head, or her heart, or any other part of her body.

Estrella pushed back from the table and stood. 'I should go. It's late. I've still so much to do.'

He rose, too. 'What else can I do? I know there must be more.'

He probably could do more. He could probably buy her a screening. He could buy her an audience, too. But she couldn't ask him. It was dangerous. Wrong. 'If you want to help, support Relief Now. It's the nonprofit group Allie worked with and I'm sure they'd welcome a donation.'

Carlo walked her outside and put her into the back of a cab, but he didn't let the driver leave. Leaning into the car, Carlo's silver gaze held hers. 'I had a younger sister with special needs. She died a couple years ago but she would have liked you, Estrella. She would have liked what you're doing.' His hesitated a moment. 'I like what you're doing.'

She shook her head. She didn't know what to say. He was stirring up all her emotions again, making her feel so many contradictory things.

'Gabi was adopted,' he added quietly. 'From Romania. My mother always wanted a little girl. Gabi was her girl.'

As Carlo looked down into Estrella's face, he realised he'd fallen for her. And fallen hard. He reached out and touched her cheek. 'If you ever need someone in your corner, Estrella, you've got me.'

Her eyes filmed with tears. 'I do need—I still want a screening for *One Heart*. If you can possibly make a few calls...pull some strings...'

He straightened. 'I'll see what I can do.'

CHAPTER SIX

The screening room was dark. There was utter silence as the film ended. Estrella balled her hands against the chair's arms and tried to stifle a stab of disappointment. The audience hadn't liked it. They hadn't felt the emotion. They hadn't seen the children as she did.

The lights came up and the red auditorium remained silent, and then suddenly someone was clapping.

Many people were clapping.

Estrella felt goose bumps prickle her skin. The clapping grew louder, faster, and it was like a dull roar in her head and she didn't know what to think, or feel. They'd liked it?

A hand touched her elbow. 'Stand up,' someone said in her ear. 'They want to see you. They want to acknowledge you.'

She slowly rose to her feet and the lights rose. She felt as if she were standing in a spotlight even though there was none.

The applause still rang in Estrella's ears as the theatre emptied. She only had two wishes tonight. That Carlo would have joined her for the screening—she'd called and left him a message at his hotel but she never heard back—and that Allie would have been here tonight to see this.

Allie would have loved this. Allie deserved this.

'You've done an excellent job.'

Estrella spun to find Carlo standing in the row of seats behind her. He was in black tie and he was alone. She felt a bubble of surprise and pleasure and she drew her red silk wrap closer over her bare shoulders. 'You came.'

'Had to see it.'

Again that spike of pleasure, her chest feeling tight and the emotion so bittersweet. Carlo Gabellini was supposed to be the enemy but he didn't feel like the enemy at all any more. 'I called your hotel but when you didn't phone back...' Her voice drifted off and she blushed. She sounded like a schoolgirl.

'I had some business in Milan. Flew home for the day and only just returned this evening.'

'But you saw the film?'

'I saw it all.'

'And what do you really think?'

'It's a very powerful, very honest film.'

She knew she was beaming. She couldn't help it. She'd waited so long for this night. 'It's all Allie. She had the vision. She did the hard part. I just wanted to make sure it got seen, and it did. Thank you.'

He glanced around at the rapidly emptying theatre. 'I wish the space had been bigger. More people should have seen it.'

'Maybe some day.'

His eyes searched her face. 'You really do care for the children, don't you?'

'How can I not? They're such beautiful children and they'll have no future if they remain there. These girls deserve better. They deserve homes and education, good nutrition, and most of all—love.'

'What about adoption?'

'That's part of the goal, but it's not easy adopting children from India. There's lots of red tape, and even if one can wade through that, not all children will be adopted. So that's the second half of the equation—finding funds to help the children that can't be adopted. Trying to bring a teacher to the orphanage. Trying to get books and supplies. Trying to get medicine, food and clothes. There's so much to be done.'

Carlo's expression gentled. 'And you want to do it.'

'Yes.'

He reached out and smoothed a dark tendril back from her face. 'You can't save the world.'

She liked the feel of his hand against her face and yet his words made her heart ache. 'Why not?'

> **Fact:** Every year since 1947 the people in Oslo have given a Christmas tree to the city of Westminster. The gift is given in gratitude for Britain's help to Norway in World War II.

Thank God he didn't laugh. He simply shook his head once, a slow compassionate shake. 'Don't make me answer that. You've had a long day. Let me take you to dinner.'

She opened her mouth to refuse and then couldn't. She liked his company. She loved having him here tonight. Somehow his support mattered far more than it should and there was no way she was ready to say goodbye to him.

Lifting her head, she looked into his face. He looked so handsome, and yet so self-contained, that her heart gave a strange little lurch. She'd needed someone on her side, someone to open doors, someone to make things happen and he'd done it all.

He'd been there for her. He'd been magnificent.

For the first time she wasn't afraid of him. For the first time she wanted to just relax and be herself with him. No more worrying. No more doubting. No more struggling. Maybe dinner was just what she needed. 'Yes. Sounds great. Thank you.'

They ate at a quiet restaurant hidden behind the big hotels a couple of blocks from the crowd-jammed Croisette. After dinner they managed to avoid most of the crowds by walking back to the Carlton along the beach.

The moon shone on the water and the waves crashed foamy and white against the darker sand. Following Carlo's lead, Estrella stripped off her strappy red heels to walk barefoot next to him in the cool sand.

They walked in silence for nearly a quarter of a mile and Estrella realised she loved being with Carlo. Loved the way he made her feel— not just about life, but about herself. He seemed so strong, so grounded, so...real.

Lifting her red dress higher she felt the water circle her feet. The water was cool and her skin felt tingly. The sky here looked so big. Endless. Turning, she glanced at the glittery scene of downtown Cannes with the sea of white pavilions.

'This could be a movie,' she said, gesturing to the wide empty beach with the backdrop of the city. 'You could show a movie here on the beach, followed by a big gala. No theatre can rival this for beauty.' She laughed a little and looked at Carlo. 'Sorry. I'm talking too much.'

'Don't apologise. I like it. I like your ideas, your thoughts. I want to know everything about you.'

'But I might say too much. Or say the wrong things.'

He came to a stop next to her. 'What good is a mind if you can't have an opinion? What good is an opinion if you can't speak it?'

She smiled faintly, emotion bottled inside her. 'Be careful. I have lots of opinions.'

'Good.' He walked higher up the beach and sat down. 'Join me. And tell me about Argentina. I've never been there.'

She dropped down next to him and he peeled off his coat, settled it around her bare shoulders. She snuggled into the warm silk-lined fabric. 'This reminds me of Mar y Sierras, which translates roughly to "hills roll down to the sea".'

'Sounds romantic.'

'It can be. It's where Argentinians like to play. Like here on the French Riviera, Mar y Sierras has beautiful beaches and resorts, great nightlife, casinos. Same kind of wealthy, fashionable crowd...'

He leaned forward, cupped the back of her head and cut off her words by covering her mouth with his.

She drank in a breath at the shimmer of heat as his lips brushed hers, his skin warm and fragrant, his body hard, and she knew instinctively that this was exactly what she needed.

Her hands slid up to hold his face and she savoured the feel of him and the crisp texture of his hair.

His lips parted hers and her tummy tightened at the flick of his tongue and the pressure of his mouth against hers. The magic of the kiss wasn't technique as much as energy. The energy between them was tangible.

Carlo stretched her back against the sand and she sank into the soft grains as Carlo's black coat protected her.

His head lifted and he gazed down at her, his expression intense. 'You don't know how much I've been wanting to do that.'

'Then maybe you should do that again,' she whispered.

CHAPTER SEVEN

The emotion of the moment almost overwhelmed Estrella. 'I feel like I've been waiting forever for you,' she confessed.

Carlo settled over her, his weight balanced on his elbows, his chest just grazing hers. 'I know I have,' he answered, kissing her exposed collarbone and then the side of her neck.

She shivered at the light kiss on her neck. His lips felt so lovely against her skin. When his mouth trailed across hers, she sighed and reached up to clasp the back of his head, her fingers sinking into his crisp black hair.

'You'd better not start something you can't finish,' she whispered against his mouth.

'Perhaps we should head back?'

'To my hotel, yes.'

But en route to the Carlton they passed the Palais, with its red carpet and twenty-two stairs. All the big name directors and actors climbed those stairs. All photographers focused their lenses on the stairs.

'There they are,' Carlo said, slowing a little, his arm circling Estrella's waist. He couldn't remember when he'd last enjoyed an evening so much. He felt good when he was with her. He felt more focused and relaxed. 'The most famous steps in Cannes.'

Estrella's high heels hung from two fingers. 'It looks different without the crowds.'

'Makes you want to be part of it.'

Estrella shook her head. 'I really don't care for the celebrity part. In fact, I'm ready to move on, ready to do something for others.'

She'd surprised him. 'You'd give up modelling?'

'I've been offered a position with Relief Now.' She tucked a strand of hair behind her ear. 'I've been thinking of taking it.'

He watched her hand rake her hair back, watched the way the moonlight reflected in her eyes. He'd never get tired of looking at her. 'It's a salaried position?'

'No. But I've a little savings left and I can live off that for a year or two.'

'No more bright lights?' he asked, picturing them living quietly in his big house in Milan with weekends spent at the villa on Lake Como.

'At least, not on me.'

They reached the Carlton and climbed the front steps. Carlo walked her to the lift and she pulled him inside. 'Is there anywhere you have to be?' she asked, as the lift doors closed.

His eyes locked with hers. 'Not tonight.'

She could get lost in his eyes, lost in him. 'Then stay.'

He did.

* * *

It'd been months and months since she'd been with anyone and Estrella held her breath as Carlo slowly undressed her, unfastening the small hooks in the boned bodice of her red silk gown and pushing the full crimson fabric down over her black lace bra, down over her hips to let it pool at her feet.

His mouth followed his hands, his lips caressing her smooth shoulder, the swell of her breast, the curve of her hip. She felt so much — wanted so much — and it was thrilling to give herself over to him, to give up control and just enjoy the moment.

He knew how to make the most of the moment, too. He kissed her beneath her earlobe, and then worked his way to her breast, his tongue drawing small circles of fire over her skin. She smothered a gasp as he caught the peaked nipple between his lips, the pressure and heat of his mouth both a torture and a delight.

Being with him was erotic. Exciting. It was everything she wanted. Her body was growing hot. Her imagination was inflamed. She wanted more.

Carlo lifted his head and his light gaze met hers in the dark. He was breathing hard and his silver gaze was nearly pewter. He wanted her. He wanted everything she did.

Estrella leaned closer, brushed her breasts across his chest and then unfastened his shirt one slow button at a time.

He was watching her and she felt his keen interest as she slid the shirt from his shoulders, revealing a toned chest and a flat muscular belly. She placed her hands on his hard stomach, then delicately traced the muscles with her tongue. He was so warm and his skin smelled fragrant and he felt like satin. He was so incredibly sexy and tonight he was all hers.

She looked up at him and, with his gaze holding hers, she stripped his belt from his trousers and then unzipped them without saying a word.

There was no talking at all. It was as if they'd used all their words earlier and the silence heightened the tension, as well as the passion. She was so aware of him she felt as if she could hear his heart beat, and feel him breathe.

With his gaze still locked with hers, she gently cupped him through his briefs. He was already hard and straining and she slipped her hand beneath the white fabric to stroke him fully.

Carlo groaned deep in his throat and she stroked him again. This time she felt his taut belly contract, his lean hips rock, and for the first time in her life Estrella wanted to love a man with her hands and her mouth, she wanted to feel him and taste him. She wanted to make him hers completely.

But he wouldn't let her kneel before him.

His hands lifted her to her feet and he carried her to the bed.

There was something intensely alive between them, something that couldn't be defined by the mind or with words. And when Carlo lowered his head to kiss her— really kiss her with his lips and his tongue—she knew she'd never really made love before. She'd had sex and she'd felt pleasure but it'd never been love, never been close to the joy of this.

And it was joy to be close to someone and to feel so good. It was wonderful to feel as if something mattered and life made sense. To feel empowered by love...

Carlo shifted his weight, moving between her thighs, and with a smooth thrust he entered her body and helplessly she tightened around him, her breath catching in her throat, her skin feverishly hot, sensitive to the slightest touch.

Their lovemaking was slow and intense. There was no pressure, no race, nothing to be won or gained. It was just touch, it was just sensation, it was just the two of them together, alone.

When Estrella felt the pleasure building and the tension return, sensation turning sharp and strong, she curled her arms around Carlo's shoulders and buried her face against his warm damp skin and gave herself totally to him, not just her body, but her heart.

She'd never thought she'd feel this way about anyone, and yet this was love, she was certain of it. After a lifetime of fragments and broken pieces, Carlo made her feel complete.

* * *

Estrella woke early in the morning to Carlo's

caress and they made love again, and later when they were both spent, Estrella propped her chin on her hand and looked down at him.

'You never talk about your life,' she said, suddenly feeling very serious. 'You never talk about your family, or your past loves.'

'My family's huge. I have three brothers... all working in Italy and dozens of cousins.' He shrugged. 'And until you, there hasn't ever been a love. There have been women. And lovers. But never a love.'

Her heart did a funny double beat. 'I feel the same way about you.'

> **Tip:** For an unusual and stylish Christmas focal point, pile pinecones into baskets, along with a few that you've sprayed gold or some pretty baubles.

Carlo reached out to cup her cheek, loving the shape of her face, the intelligence in her hazel-green eyes. She was everything he'd ever wanted in a woman—and more. 'What do you want more than anything right now?'

'Save all the beautiful babies I can in Tamil Nadu.'

She was going to break his heart, he thought, leaning forward to kiss her lips. 'After that?' he murmured.

'Get *One Heart* distributed around the world. I want everyone to know about the orphanage.'

He kissed her again. 'And so it shall be done.'

Later that morning they went for a drive,

131

leaving noisy crowded Cannes behind and taking a road high into the mountains, giving them a spectacular view of the Riviera.

Carlo stopped in Mougins, an old hilltop town with ramparts dating from the fifteenth century. Once parked, they left the car and walked across a meadow filled with wildflowers to a crumbling stone wall.

They sat down on the wall and Estrella leaned against Carlo. 'This is lovely. It's so peaceful here.'

Carlo gazed down at Estrella, her long dark hair draped across one shoulder, and his chest felt hot and tight. He'd never felt this way before. He knew he'd never feel this way about anyone again.

He turned her around so she faced him. His eyes searched hers. God, he loved her. He couldn't imagine life without her. Cupping her face in his hands he kissed her. 'Marry me.'

CHAPTER EIGHT

'Marry me,' Carlo repeated urgently.

They were, Estrella thought, the sweetest words she'd ever heard. For him to know her goals, her dream, her passion and still want her—it was remarkable. Her eyes burned and a massive lump filled her throat. 'I can't.'

He held her before him, his hands on her upper arms. 'Why not?'

'I'd be a terrible wife.'

'No!'

She stood up on tiptoe and gently kissed him, her lips brushing his. 'Yes. Especially to a Gabellini. Gabellinis are wealthy and powerful

and extremely prominent—you're like the Galváns in Argentina—but it's everything I don't want. Everything I can't be any more.'

'*Cara*, darling...'

'No.' Her eyes burned like fire and it was all she could do to hold the tears in check. 'Please, don't argue. It'll only make it worse. We have different goals, Carlo. We're heading in different directions.'

* * *

Carlo drove them back to Cannes and the tension during the return drive was unbearable. Pulling up at the Carlton, Carlo parked and turned to her, his features grim. 'I don't understand why you don't think we'll work.'

'What we have won't last. It can't.' Her eyes felt as gritty as sand. 'In less than a week Cannes will be transformed again. The posters will come down, the red carpet rolled up, the crowds dispersed. We're the same. We're part of the magic here, but this isn't the real world. At least, it's not my real world. My world is in Tamil Nadu.'

She saw him blanch, saw the fear in his eyes. 'You don't have to go to India to help the children,' he said tersely. 'You can raise funds here. You can increase public awareness without putting yourself in the line of fire.'

She knew he was referring to Allie. 'If I don't go I won't know the money is reaching the children. I have to be certain the girls are getting proper care. I can't just hope everything will turn out right. I must make sure it does.'

His jaw hardened. His silver gaze grew

flinty. 'You won't even give us a chance.'

The first tear fell and Estrella dashed it away. 'I can't, Carlo, but I do love you. I'll always love you.'

'You're saying goodbye, then?'

Oh, she hated those words and she hated them said like that. He made it sound as if this was easy. It wasn't easy. It felt like hell but she couldn't give up on the girls. She'd made a promise. 'Not goodbye.' Her voice cracking with emotion, 'What about *au revoir*? Until the next time?'

'No. I hate it. I won't say it.'

'Then don't.' She pressed her mouth to his, closed her eyes, and told herself to remember what it felt like being loved like this. She told herself to remember his strength, his warmth and his tremendous generosity.

Fighting tears, she turned her head and whispered in his ear. 'I will never forget you. I will never forget what you've done for me and the children of Tamil Nadu.'

Before he could answer she slipped from the car and disappeared into her hotel, blinking back tears as she ran.

* * *

Late that night two envelopes appeared beneath Estrella's door. She carried them to her bed.

The first envelope was of a heavy cream paper and she drew out a stiff cream invitation. *You are cordially invited to join Integro Investment Bank for the Premiere of One Heart, 7 o'clock, The Riviera.*

The gala event Carlo had promised.

Hands shaking, she opened the second envelope and discovered a first-class ticket to New Delhi. It was, she noted with fresh tears welling in her eyes, just one way.

The next evening Estrella dressed for the screening with infinite care, doing her hair and applying her make-up as if she were girding herself for battle. And in a way, she was. She was preparing to face Carlo one last time before leaving him later tonight.

Looking at her pale reflection in the bathroom she knew it would be hell tonight. Being with him and yet not being with him was as cruel a punishment as she could imagine.

She reached up and adjusted the strap of her gown. The fabric was a nude satin with an overlay of small violet flowers, the flowers speckled with clear sequins. It was an extravagant gown, a high-voltage Hollywood type of gown, but tonight Estrella had to play the part of the glamorous model one last time. Tonight she had to shine for the photographers and the press and make sure *One Heart* got all the attention it possibly could.

Carlo had sent his limousine for her and en route to the Riviera she saw bright white spotlights streak the sky. It wasn't until the limousine stopped at the beach that she discovered the spotlights were for the premiere and they were drawing a crowd.

She was awed. Carlo had thought of

everything. A dozen flashbulbs popped in her eyes as she stepped on to the red carpet, the press converging just as they did for the big studio premieres.

How had he organised all this in three days? He'd put together the screening, the party, the press, even the red carpet—for her.

She nearly lost her composure then. She was so grateful for all that he'd done, and so overwhelmed by his support. She'd never met a man like Carlo before and doubted she ever would again.

Carlo met her inside the white pavilion tent on the sand. The screening was black-tie and again he wore his tuxedo.

Estrella felt her heart turn over as she looked at him. He was so big, so imposing, so fiercely protective of her dream.

'You look gorgeous,' she said, resting her hand on his sleeve and rising to kiss his cheek.

He turned his head and caught the kiss on his mouth. 'I love you.'

Her eyes burned and she felt the ache in her chest like the tide of the sea. It was pulling on her, sucking her in, and yet she couldn't give in. As soon as she thought of the girls, she knew she had to go, knew she had a job to do.

'I love you, too,' she whispered before she was surrounded by a circle of international buyers and pulled in the opposite direction to Carlo.

* * *

Later, the big white tent became a massive movie screen and the guests in glittering evening dress sat down in chairs and on blankets spread across the sand. Then the lights strung across the inside of the tent dimmed and a projector was turned on, showing the first of two reels of film.

By the time the screening ended, the documentary had been picked up by a legion of networks, independent distributors and the largest cable companies in the United States. Everyone who was anyone had attended the premiere and there was talk of the film being nominated for an Oscar and possibly shown at next year's Sundance Film Festival.

The evening had been a huge success but, like everything, the party eventually ended. The guests departed. The tent came down and Estrella returned to her hotel where she changed into travelling clothes, packed her bags and paid her bill.

At the Nice airport, Estrella checked in and cleared security. It was while waiting at the gate that she spotted a familiar dark head bent over a newspaper.

Estrella's jaw dropped. Carlo? At the airport?

'What are you doing here?' she demanded, confronting him just as the announcement was made that the aeroplane would begin boarding in just a moment.

He looked up from the paper, feigning

shock. 'My God, Estrella, what are you doing here?'

'Don't start with me. What are you doing here, and where are you going?'

He rose. 'Well, I'm getting on a plane, and I'm going to India.'

'You can't! That's where I'm going.'

He whistled. 'Fate.'

'No, it's not fate. It's wrong.'

'It's not wrong.' Carlo held out his airline ticket. He had a seat assignment. It was the seat next to hers. 'I have a ticket, I have a seat, and I'm going.'

'But...why?'

'Because you're going. And I want to be there. Someone's got to keep an eye on you.'

It wasn't because he didn't trust her. It was because he *cared*. He loved her. Even though he'd said the words before, she felt it for the first time, felt it in her middle, in her bones, in her heart. He'd be with her, stand by her, and after a lifetime of standing alone it was heaven.

Yet still, the knowledge bowled her over. She knew what he was giving up. Knew the sacrifices he'd make. 'But your company. And your family...'

'Doesn't matter. I'm doing this for you, Estrella, but I'm also doing it for myself. If I can help the children, I want to.'

Estrella's eyes filled with tears. 'Where we're going there are no luxury hotels.'

He reached out and drew her into his arms, his hands curving in the small of her back. 'I understand, *cara*. I can handle a sleeping bag, a mosquito net, and bottled water.'

'So you know there'll be bugs.'

'Yes. There'll be lots of bugs.' Then he smiled, a small crooked smile. 'But I think I could handle a swarm of locusts if it means I get to spend the next year of my life with you.'

Her smile faltered. 'Just a year?'

'That depends on whether or not you'll marry me.'

'Yes!' She slid her arms around his neck and lifted her mouth to his. 'Carlo Gabellini,
I want to marry you. I want to love you. I want to spend the rest of my life with you.'

He smiled before brushing his lips across hers. 'Can I get that in writing?'

Estrella laughed, her heart lighter than it had been in years. 'It's not necessary. We don't stand a chance. We're meant to be together. It's fate.' ∎

The Sheikh's Chosen Queen is Jane Porter's sultry new Modern Romance title which is available in January 2008.

Celebrating the

Advent

Christmas can be something of a balancing act—there are so many friends and relatives to see, but just one special day. This year take the pressure off yourself by celebrating the whole of the festive season. You don't need to restrict yourself to just Christmas Day when there are plenty of opportunities to have a special celebration with those you can't be with on the big day itself. We've got some suggestions for making the whole of December a time for fun and festivities, and ensuring you spend time with everyone who matters to you.

Advent begins with Advent Sunday, which falls on the nearest Sunday to 30th November, marking the beginning of the new year of the Christian Church and the church season that leads to Christmas Day. Of course, nowadays Advent is very much associated with Advent calendars—chocolate or otherwise! So Advent Sunday might be the perfect time to meet up with the children of friends, or nieces and nephews that you won't see on Christmas Day. It's a really easy day to make child-friendly and fun-filled.

Here are our top tips for making Advent Sunday a treat:

- Light a candle! Candles are traditionally lit on each Sunday of advent, so get the kids involved in a special candle-lighting ceremony.

- Make a personalised Advent calendar for the kids:

  - Hang 24 small paper bags/gift bags/sandwich bags from a piece of string using string or clothes pegs.

136

festive season

Fill each bag with a little present—a 50p piece, a small bar of chocolate, hairclips, stamps, stickers and so on.

- If you don't have time to make a personal Advent calendar, wrap up one of the lovely shop-bought ones that are available—they'll still love it.

- How about making the first mince pies of the season on Advent Sunday? Just buy some ready-to-roll pastry and a couple of interesting Christmas cutters to get your special guests involved.

The Winter Solstice

The Winter Solstice—the shortest day of the year—has been celebrated since ancient times as the day that heralds the return of the sun. Even today, people gather at sites such as Stonehenge to mark this day. We think that it's a great excuse for a more grown-up get-together. Ask friends or relatives who you won't see over Christmas to come over for a dinner party, serve them a traditional roast and make the most of the longest night!

Try these ideas for making your evening truly special:

- Serve a signature drink when your guests arrive, such as a champagne cocktail:

  - Place a brown sugar lump in the bottom of a champagne flute and drizzle a few drops of Angostura Bitters over the top.

  - Add a splash of brandy.

  - Fill the glass three-quarters full with champagne or good-quality fizz and enjoy!

- Dress the house with lots of white flowers, white balloons and pussy willow branches, for that winter wonderland look.

- At each guest's place, make sure there's a little white chocolate to welcome them when they sit down.

- For dessert, serve your guests Yule log. In ancient pagan ritual, the Yule log was lit on the eve of Winter Solstice and burned for twelve hours.

The Twelve Days of Christmas

The Twelve Days of Christmas start with Christmas Day and finish on the eve of the Epiphany on 5th January. They symbolise the time it took for the Three Kings to arrive in Bethlehem from the East. This period was traditionally celebrated with a lot of feasting and fun, so take your inspiration from days gone by. We're not suggesting that you celebrate all twelve days, unless you're feeling particularly festive! But picking one of the days to share with friends or family can perk up that period between Christmas and New Year.

The Carol

Use the Christmas song 'The Twelve Days of Christmas' as a starting point for a fantastic festive celebration and plan a party:

A Partridge in a Pear Tree:

It may be ambitious to get hold of one of these! But bowls of pears for your guests to tuck into will look very stylish.

Three French Hens:

Serve your guests a delicious roasted chicken—it'll make a welcome change from all that turkey. Pep it up by rubbing some ground coriander, paprika and cumin on the bird before you roast it for a delicate spicy flavour.

Five Gold Rings:

Use this verse to inspire your party décor. Gold paper napkins, napkin holders and gold candles are widely available at Christmas, and pine cones look fantastic sprayed gold. And with the Olympic year coming up, why not use the five Olympic rings as part of your look?

Fancy Dress:

Ask your guests to use the song as a starting point and to come in festive fancy dress. Be prepared for lots of Lords a-Leaping...

Modern and Ancient Traditions

The Twelve Days continue to be celebrated today across the world, and we think that honouring some of these traditions, even in a small way can give you the perfect excuse to spend time with those who matter to you.

Tortell des Reis

- This is a magnificent cake that hails from Catalonia. It is normally an O-shaped pastry that is filled with marzipan and topped with glazed fruit, which is traditionally eaten on the Feast of the Epiphany—6th January.

- We suggest that you use this as an excuse to catch up with friends. Invite them over for a slice of cake—your favourite, or a Tortell if you can track it down in a deli and serve with a lovely glass of wine. You don't have to make a big fuss to make an occasion special.

The Forgotten Friend

- It happens to all of us—we receive a gift that we weren't expecting, or we just plain forget to get one, but the Twelve Days of Christmas were traditionally the time that gifts were given and received.

- So why not wrap up a present, attach an appropriate verse from the song, and explain that you are going back to Britain's traditional Christmas roots!

Ed Gardener

Our favourite gardener returns with some fantastic tips and ideas on how to make your garden — however big or small — really beautiful this year.

Dear Reader

While writing this I am aware that the seasons (according to the experts!) are changing. In the past in early February, we would be expecting hard frost and

snowfall. Today, many bulbs are in flower—snowdrops, crocus, and early flowering shrubs such as forsythia and camellia are all breaking into flower. As gardeners we must be aware of changing weather patterns and plan our year accordingly.

Trees make a difference

I will begin by encouraging you to plant a tree for 2008. Ideally, if you have the space available in your garden you will plant there and watch it grow. With the main planting season from October through to March we have a huge choice of native and hybrid species from which to make our pick. Some I would recommend for smaller gardens are crataegus (flowering thorns) and malus (ornamental crab apple) which both have abundant spring flowers and ornamental fruit in the autumn, or Acers (Japanese maples) with their dazzling autumn leaf colours. To combine flowers and fruit, why not plant some fruit trees. Even with

imited space they can be grown on a wall or fence.

For those of you without gardens you could approach your local authority to plant or sponsor a tree in your local park or arboretum. These are often planted 'in memoriam' but how much better to watch it grow in your lifetime? On the same note, you may also be able to rent an allotment, and with a little time and effort you can reap rewards and gain friends along the way!

Water saving tips

With our recent dry summers we must look at ways of collecting rainwater for use in the garden. Water butts connected to downpipes are quite easy to install, so use your garage,

garden shed and greenhouse where possible. Do keep the water butt covered to stop two-legged and four-legged friends from falling in! Using drought-resistant plants and mulching materials, such as mushroom compost, ornamental bark and coloured gravels, can save on water and maintenance.

Think about reducing your planting of summer bedding, which requires constant watering and feeding. You could use perennial plants to give you year-round colour. I recommend bergenia, campanula, delphinium, hellebores, lupins and sedum.

Nowadays people downsize a house — why not downsize your lawn? It will cut down on time consuming lawn-mowing and watering. Personally I like a small lawn, but some people have replaced their lawns completely with paving or ornamental gravels. This can be quite effective if broken up with planters and containers.

Maximise your space

For those of you with limited space, or the age-old gardeners' back problems, think about constructing some raised beds, with the growing area at waist level. Many plants can be grown without bending or kneeling, and raised beds can make a space look bigger. Consider a small area for herbs, which will provide colour and scent as well as being useful in the kitchen, and salad crops can also be grown in raised beds throughout the summer.

coriander

rosemary

parsley

Taking care of business — the natural way

Gardeners constantly battle with weeds and pests. Weeding should be done frequently—before the weeds have a chance to seed. The garden hoe and your fingers are the best tools for this job. Vigilance is required to keep pests under control—picking off any damaging pests and using a light spray of water to remove any eggs. Damaged and diseased leaves should also be removed. With all the current concern about using chemicals and pesticides, make 2008 your year to garden as organically as you can.

Finally

I would like to dedicate this column to my father, who passed away in 2007 at the grand old age of 94. He spent all of his leisure time in his garden providing fruit and vegetables for his large family and friends all the year round. He pickled his own onions and produced enough runner beans for the table and the freezer, as well as green bean chutney for the winter months. Much of my gardening experience came from working alongside him.

Ed Gardener

Scrambled Eggs

Kate Mayhew

'You can't unscramble an egg, dear,' her mother had said. 'In time, you'll be glad about it,' she'd insisted. 'In time, you'll be grateful for scrambled eggs...'

'Mum...!' Helen had choked between sobs. 'Could you leave the scrambled eggs out of it this time? *Please?*'

For as far back as Helen could remember, her mother had brought scrambled eggs into the equation every time something bad happened. The day her cousin had decapitated Eddy-the-Teddy and relieved him

of his stuffing... *You can't unscramble an egg*. The day her school skirt had fallen down around her ankles in the middle of that final-year prize-giving ceremony... *You can't unscramble an egg*. And, yes, on the day her husband had left her, telling her he didn't love her—that he wasn't sure he'd ever loved her ... *You can't unscramble an egg*.

Helen had cried for a week—a week in which a single, desolate thought had unfurled itself inside her heart: She would never, *ever* be grateful for scrambled eggs.

* * *

'Let's go for Fire-Engine Red today,' Gloria said with a wink.

'Fire-Engine Red it is,' said Helen, flipping open her mother's vanity case and fishing out the bright red polish. She always did Mum's nails during the chemotherapy sessions. It took Gloria's mind off things.

The American doctor was standing near the window, but Helen could see that he was smiling. And that made her smile, too. She liked that he had a soft spot for her mother.

'Okay, Mrs Adams,' he said, lifting his head from Gloria's medical notes, and slotting them back into their folder. 'You're all set. I'll leave you to it.'

'Thank you, Doctor,' Gloria said, all gracious, elegant smiles.

'Yes, thanks...' Helen echoed, blushing slightly when the doctor looked directly at her—and feeling suddenly very ungracious and inelegant in her slouchy jeans and over-sized sweater.

'He's so handsome, isn't he?' Gloria whispered after he'd gone, her eyes twinkling mischief. 'I think he looks like George Clooney.'

'Mum!' Helen said, trying to stifle a laugh. 'He's your doctor!'

'I know, lucky me!' Gloria trilled. Helen's heart squeezed. Her mother was battling cancer, and still her glass was half full.

'Come on. Let's get you comfortable.' She settled her mother gently against the starchy hospital pillows.

'He's the sort of man I'd like to see you with, you know,' Gloria went on in hushed, conspiratorial tones. 'Why don't you ask him

on a date? Girls do that nowadays...'

Helen looked away.

'Helen? Oh, Helen, please don't tell me you still think about that brute of an ex-husband?'

'Not really...' *More than she should.*

'Good. Because he was cruel, and he was a cad—and you deserve better.'

Helen swallowed the brittle lump in her throat. 'I loved him, Mum,' she said, dropping her lashes, biting the inside of her cheek. Refusing to cry.

'I know you did, darling,' her mother said, wrapping her too-thin arms around her daughter. 'I know you did. But one day it will make sense,' she added softly, taking Helen's face in her hands. 'One day, life will show you why it happened. One day, my love, you'll be grateful for scrambled eggs. I promise.'

Helen nodded and tried for a smile. She wanted to believe it. She wanted to believe that things happened for a reason. That there'd be sunshine after the rain. But in her heart she knew it wasn't true. In her heart, she knew there were some promises that even her mother couldn't keep.

* * *

December 21st. Cold. Glassy. Christmassy. Gloria's birthday. The Victorian cemetery was beautiful—magical—in the wintry morning light. A dusting of snow covered the headstones. The trees made bare, vulnerable silhouettes against the white-grey sky.

Helen crouched at the graveside to arrange the winter tulips she'd brought. They'd been Gloria's favourites.

'Happy Birthday, Mum,' she murmured, resting her hand on the cold stone. 'I love you.'

'Oh. I'm sorry, I—'

Helen straightened and whirled around, startled by the voice. And then her heart skipped a beat. It was the American doctor. The George Clooney one. They'd crossed paths a few times during Mum's treatment. Gloria had liked him. He'd known how to make her smile.

Helen's mind reeled back to the day her mother had snagged him into choosing her nail colour. 'Help me choose, Doctor!' she'd implored in her sing-song voice. And the doctor had furrowed his handsome brow and studied the collection of bottles for several long minutes before announcing, 'Gloria,' in a mock-serious voice, 'it has to be Vaudeville Pink.' And that had made both Gloria and Helen laugh.

'Doctor...'

'James,' he interrupted gently, taking a step closer and holding out his hand. 'It's James.' She took his hand and they locked eyes. 'Good to see you, Helen,' he said, and a little burst of warmth flared in her chest. *He remembered her name.*

'I didn't mean to intrude. I hope you don't—'

'No! Gosh, of course not! Did you, um... Did you know it was Mum's birthday?' He smiled at that, and she felt her tummy flip.

'Gloria and I—we got to know each other over the months. I think she felt sorry for me, to tell you the truth. American in London... Fish out of water, and all that...' A muscle tightened along his jaw. 'She helped me through a difficult time. She was a good friend.' His voice trailed off, and Helen felt a stab of sadness. Gloria had told her his story.

'You see, Helen?' Mum had said knowingly. *'You're not the only thirty-something in London with a broken heart...'*

'Before your mother died,' James continued, 'she asked me if I'd visit her on her birthday. Asked if I'd come for the morning bells...' He glanced up at the old church tower. 'I guess she liked bells.'

'I guess she did,' Helen said with a small, private smile as she guessed something else, too. *Her mother. She'd set this up.*

James placed his flowers next to Helen's, and they stood together in the gently fluttering snow, listening to the tinny, bright-sounding bells ring out across the cemetery.

* * *

'You're shivering,' James said, when a long time had passed and the cemetery had fallen silent again. 'And you have snowflakes on your eyelashes,' he added, with a smile warm enough to melt them. 'Here.' He shrugged out of his coat and draped it around her shoulders.

'Thank you...' Helen hesitated. Pressed her

lips together for several seconds. Several seconds was really all she needed.

'James?'

James lifted his eyebrows.

'Would you let me buy you breakfast?'

His smile broadened. 'Sure.'

* * *

They wound their way through Bloomsbury until they reached a tiny American diner tucked away in a side street. It was cosy. Homely. Tinsel-decorated booths hugged the walls, and a mouth-watering coffee-and-pancakes aroma wafted from the kitchen. James lifted his coat from her shoulders, then helped her out of her own. When his fingers brushed the backs of her arms, a dozen butterflies took flight in her stomach.

'Coffee?' The waitress asked as she guided them to a booth.

'Please. *Lots* of coffee. We're freezing.' James said. Helen watched him while he studied the menu and ordered two house breakfasts.

'Better?' he quizzed, settling his dark, sincere eyes on her again.

'Better.' She smiled, feeling warmth spreading back into her bones.

'So...' He paused. 'How are you...? How've you been....?'

He was the first person to ask her that. In the three months since her mother's death, everyone seemed to have developed an inexplicable interest in the weather. And it was the strangest thing. She barely knew him — yet she felt she'd known him all her life. There was no need to lie. No need to pretend

everything was fine. No need to pretend the world was still the same.

She opened her mouth to speak. Felt grief rush to the surface.

'I miss her...' she whispered, her face crumpling, her eyes filling. 'I miss her so much...'

James reached across the table and took her hand. 'I know.'

It was all he said. It was all he needed to say. When she looked into his face — into his eyes — she saw that he understood. And that he cared.

They sat quietly, her hand in his, for a long time. Something was happening. She felt it. *Did he?* Something magical? Wonderful? Unexpected?

Just then the waitress reappeared at their booth.

'Sorry to interrupt you guys,' she said. 'I forgot to ask... How d'you like your eggs?'

James looked at Helen, and Helen looked at James. She saw his lips curve into a smile. Felt tingles along her spine.

'Scrambled, right, Helen?' James said, giving her hand a reassuring squeeze. Smiling all the way to his George Clooney eyes.

'Scrambled.' Helen nodded, beaming her brightest smile at him — and sending her beloved mum a silent thank you.

'Most definitely scrambled.' ■

ARROW WORDS

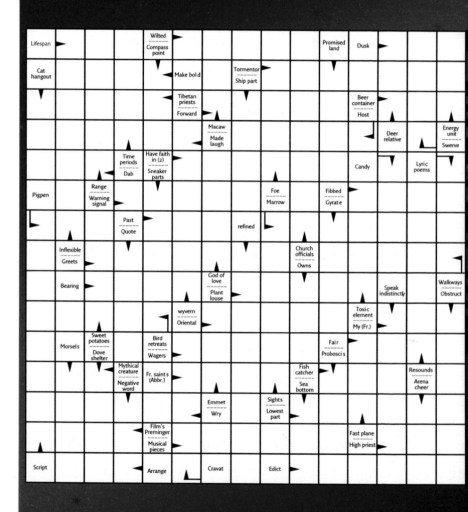

CONNECT-IT
WORLD FAMOUS

Each line in the puzzle below has three clues and three answers. The last letter in the first answer on each line is the first letter of the second answer, and so on. The connecting letter is outlined, giving you the correct number of letters for each answer (the answers in line 1 are 4, 6 and 6 letters). The clues are numbered 1 to 8, with each number containing 3 clues for the 3 answers on the line. But here's the catch! The clues are not in order—so the first clue in the line is not necessarily for the first answer. Good luck!

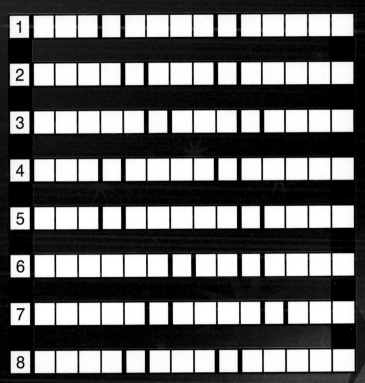

CLUES

1. Poise. English novelist. Entreaty.   2. Happy. Out of fashion. Italian poet.
3. German composer. Mid-day meal. Rebuff.   4. French painter. Satire. Anchovy.
5. Mountain range. Songbird. Irish novelist.   6. Short letter. American naturalist. Void.
7. Spanish explorer. Vow. Openly frank.   8. Agile. Musical instrument. Greek muse.

HITORI

To solve a Hitori puzzle, shade the squares so that the numbers only appear once in each column or row. Not every number needs to appear in each column or row... but remember, they cannot appear more than once! Shaded squares cannot be next to each other in a row or a column. Unshaded squares must be connected to another unshaded square either vertically or horizontally.

3	3	2	4	3	6	2	6
4	6	2	7	3	5	5	8
5	7	6	8	2	2	2	1
7	2	6	7	7	5	1	4
3	5	6	6	2	4	4	4
7	4	5	2	1	4	8	3
2	4	8	5	1	7	7	6
8	8	1	1	1	3	7	6

WORD SEARCH

GEMS

```
R  T  O  D  I  R  E  P  N  Z  B  S  E  I  B  U  R
L  Z  M  C  B  Q  S  P  I  N  E  L  Y  J  Z  N  K
A  B  P  W  R  K  B  R  Z  E  Z  D  X  W  D  E  M
N  Q  G  Y  Q  T  C  T  M  N  R  Q  Y  Q  S  J  X
Q  N  U  C  Y  O  O  E  L  A  G  G  N  I  M  A  D
D  K  L  A  N  J  R  P  S  D  B  N  O  P  X  S  Y
Z  M  W  T  M  A  N  T  A  Y  M  U  T  G  Y  P  M
B  E  R  Y  L  A  P  V  E  Z  Q  X  T  L  N  E  E
K  L  B  D  G  E  R  P  E  R  D  P  D  G  O  R  N
V  N  W  N  A  N  L  I  U  D  I  F  H  T  D  H  I
A  Y  T  R  R  N  M  T  N  V  A  H  X  T  R  L  L
C  G  L  H  N  L  R  B  F  E  M  J  P  H  A  G  A
K  S  A  R  E  H  F  K  R  P  O  J  R  P  S  P  M
Z  L  W  T  T  K  N  N  X  J  N  E  O  V  A  X  R
T  K  C  F  E  X  W  R  R  G  D  C  M  N  D  S  U
M  M  T  D  T  S  Y  H  T  E  M  A  R  A  L  Z  O
V  S  T  O  N  E  W  T  V  M  K  K  M  C  C  J  T
```

AGATE	JADE	SARD
AMETHYST	JASPER	SARDONYX
AQUAMARINE	ONYX	SPINEL
BERYL	OPAL	STONE
CAMEO	PEARLS	TOPAZ
DIAMOND	PERIDOT	TOURMALINE
EMERALD	RUBIES	TURQUOISE
GARNET	SAPPHIRE	ZIRCON

KRISS KROSS FILL-IN

HERBS, SPICES & MORE!

4 letter words
Alfa
Mace
Mint

5 letter words
Emmer
Thyme

6 letter words
Fennel
Sesame
Sorrel

7 letter words
Caraway
Comfrey
Oregano
Succory

8 letter words
Hog's-bean
Rosemary
Waybread

10 letter words
Lemon thyme
Motherwort
Watercress

11 letter words
Hedge hyssop
Winter green

SUDOKU 1

To solve the Sudoku puzzle, each row, column and
box must contain the numbers 1 to 9.

2	4					8		
							7	
5	9	6						4
							6	9
				5				
			9	7	3			1
			8	9			3	
	3						5	8
7			4		2			

CROSSWORD

Copyright ©2007 PuzzleJunction.c

ACROSS

1. That which may be hard to accomplish
6. Request assistance (3,1,6)
13. The inner self (Jungian psychology)
14. Actors
15. Sticker
16. Snared at the wrong moment (6,2,3,3)
17. Anew
18. Absent
20. Head waiter or naval skipper

22. Soups or stews
27. Traverse a bridge
28. Varieties
29. Second smallest planet
30. Follow the action (2,5,4,3,5)
34. Nigerian monetary unit
35. Distinguish oneself
37. Mexican dish
38. Doglike nocturnal mammals

39. German city
40. Excessive fervour
43. Aircraft storage unit
45. Take a look to make sure (3,3,8)
49. Band together
50. Mistake
51. Hot pepper dish
52. Carried out with no problem (6,4)
53. Despite anything to the contrary (3,3,4)

DOWN

1. Odds against it (1,3,6)
2. Goodbye
3. Detest
4. Hold on to
5. Expel
7. Vertical support post
8. Likewise
9. Self-restraint in the expression of emotion (1,5,5,3)
10. Colourless gas
11. Be the boss (3,3,4)

12. A source of difficulty (1,6,6,2,4)
19. Acknowledge an indiscretion
21. Cupid's weapon
23. Largest mammal (4,5)
24. Distinct, to the ear (2,5,2,1,4)
25. Retaliated
26. Marrow
31. Motif
32. Free, as a gift (2,3,5)
33. Human dynamo (4,2,4)

36. Lizard
41. Common European bird
42. Prophet
44. Tacks
46. Majestic
47. True heath
48. Water hole

SUDOKU 2

To solve the Sudoku puzzle, each row, column and
box must contain the numbers 1 to 9.

	7				3	4		6
		3	2	6				
				7	5			
				2		1		5
		9	7			8		4
	3							
	5		1	9		7		
1					8			9
	4					5		

KAKURO

To solve a Kakuro fill the grid with numbers so that each block of spaces adds up to the total in the box above or to the left of it. You can only use the digits 1-9 and you must not use the same digit twice in a single block of spaces. (The same digit may occur more than once in a row or column, but it must be in a separate block.)

Lessons in Love
Claire Baxter

Laura Catalano glanced around the classroom once more, checking that everything was in order. Nearly time for the last appointment of the day and she'd done all she could.

She'd written a note in Matt's diary herself. She knew Matt's father was a busy man, but that was no excuse for a lack of interest in his son's education. In the months she'd been Matt's teacher, she hadn't seen his father at all.

Laura sighed. Short of a summons from the school principal, she'd done everything to ensure Craig Sebastian would come to see her. She'd allocated the last session of the night to him. All he had to do was show up.

She rose and peered through the window. She'd wait.

Craig's mind wandered as he cooked dinner for Matt and himself. Cooked? Huh! Baked beans on toast could hardly be called cooking but it was the best he could manage after the day he'd had. Even now he should be at a client meeting but he'd had to collect Matt from his after-school carer—much to his boss's disgust.

Besides, he was no match for a five-year-old when it came to arguing about food and Matt's favourites changed more often than the weather. He put the plate down in front of Matt, who was busy emptying his school bag on to the table.

'Come on, Mattie, eat up.'

Craig watched his son shovel food into his mouth and mentally postponed the table

manners lecture. It was the least of his problems tonight.

Sighing, he retrieved the lunch box that had tumbled on to the floor and flipped open the lid to see Matt's healthy lunch, untouched.

> **Tip:** Never mix daffodils with other cut flowers — they produce a deadly toxin that will kill off all the other blooms!

'What did you eat today?'

'Miss Cat gave me a sandwich.'

Craig frowned. 'Who?'

'My teacher. You know, Dad. I told her you forgot to make my lunch.'

'But I didn't.'

Matt grimaced. 'I don't like egg sandwiches any more. They smell.'

Great. Now Matt's teacher would have him down as a neglectful parent. Craig rubbed his throbbing forehead. It was all right for his boss—he had a wife to take care of this sort of thing. *He* didn't have that luxury.

But Matt didn't have a mother, Craig reminded himself.

She'd abandoned Matt. He still didn't understand how she could have done it. She could have divorced him but remained a part of Matt's life. She didn't have to disappear.

It wasn't the time to think about Rebecca's vanishing act with their neighbour, a man he'd considered a friend, so he shook his head and bent to pick up Matt's school diary. He flicked it open with a guilty pang. He was supposed to read the diary every day but if he managed it once a week, it was a good week.

He found the right page and tensed at the sight of adult handwriting. He groaned as he read the note.

'There's a message about going to school tonight.'

'Mmm.' Matt nodded and swallowed a mouthful of beans. 'Miss Cat said you need to go.'

Just great. What about the work he was supposed to catch up on tonight?

'She said I can play in the hall.'

This new teacher sounded determined to see him. Was there a problem at school? Something he'd know about if he'd had the time to pay attention?

* * *

Laura was reading her notes again to take her mind off the clock. She had no way of knowing whether he was coming but she wouldn't leave until she was absolutely sure he wouldn't turn up.

At a sudden noise in the corridor, her gaze shot to the doorway. A man filled the space. Not just any man but one who was the image of Matt. The same dark-blond hair, the same pale blue eyes and the same heartbreaking expression that she'd seen on Matt's face when she'd first met him. Lost. As if he had no idea what he was doing in her classroom.

With his hands jammed into his pockets, Craig Sebastian darted a glance around the room till he caught sight of her at one of the child-size tables.

He didn't look at her face at first but his gaze homed in on the old silver pendant at her throat. His mouth opened and he leaned forward but was either unable or unwilling to walk into the room.

'Hello?' Her voice vibrated with uncertainty but the single word was enough to make his eyes jerk to her face.

* * *

Laura.

Craig switched off the engine but continued to sit in the car.

First the necklace, then the voice and, finally, that face. The face he'd fallen in love with at first sight all those years ago at university.

He'd been besotted with Laura. He'd wanted to marry her, but he'd held off asking the question, wanting to gain professional qualifications and find a decent job before taking the all-important step. Old-fashioned, maybe, but it had felt right at the time.

He let the memories surface one by one. Beautiful memories of a gorgeous girl— sweet, generous and giving. Caring and nurturing. The love of his life.

* * *

Well, that had gone brilliantly. Laura sank into the little chair. One look at her and he'd run.

Had she aged so badly?

She made an impatient noise in her throat. It wasn't that, it was the shock. How could she blame him? *She'd* had plenty of time to get used to the idea of seeing Craig again. Two whole months.

She'd recognised his surname, of course. And once she'd seen Matt, she'd had no doubt at all that he was Craig's son. He hadn't taken after his mother in any obvious way.

At first she'd dreaded bumping into Matt's parents around the school but once she'd learned of his mother's desertion, her heart had swollen with sympathy for Matt. And for Craig.

Time had passed. Enough time for Laura to grow attached to the little boy with the familiar facial expressions. Enough time for her to know she wanted to see Craig again. She longed for much more than just seeing him.

'Um, Laura?'

She started as Jane, the teacher's assistant who'd been supervising children in the hall during parent interviews, entered with Matt at her side.

'Have you finished? Everyone else has gone home. Matt said his father would be here.' Jane glanced around the classroom.

Laura chewed her lip for a moment then hid her dismay behind a smile for her favourite little boy. She didn't want Matt to know his dad had forgotten him. She could only image how Craig would feel.

'Daddy had to rush off, Matt. I told him I'd take you home.'

'In your car, Miss Cat?'

'Yes.' Laura picked up her handbag and rummaged through it for her keys. 'Thanks, Jane.'

* * *

Craig opened his eyes. He'd expected to feel pain at the memory of Laura, not this bewildering jumble of emotions. Joy at finding her again. Hope.

And regret.

Nothing new there. He'd been living with regrets for years.

Regret that he hadn't told her how much she meant to him before it was too late.

Regret that he'd believed the rumour she'd found someone else. By the time he'd discovered the truth, Rebecca had been pregnant.

Rebecca.

There were so many regrets where Rebecca was concerned. Matt was the only good to come out of their relationship. He didn't regret having Matt for a minute—

Matt!

He slammed his palm against his forehead. He'd left his son at the school. In his haste, he fumbled with the keys and before he could start the car, a vehicle turned in behind his.

He got out of the car and for the second time in one evening found himself face to face with Laura.

'I've brought Matt home as we arranged,' she said brightly as she opened a door to let his son out of the car.

Grateful to her for covering for him, he ruffled Matt's hair and had to swallow hard before he could speak. 'Thank you. Would you like a cup of coffee?' he said at last.

'Yes, please.'

> ❄ **Tip:** Do you want a more sophisticated look for your house this Christmas? Then choose a theme and take it through every room!

He led the way into his renovated cottage. After sending Matt to change for bed and ushering Laura into the lounge, he hurriedly made two mugs of coffee. When he carried them through to the other room, the sight of her sitting on his sofa made his breath jam in his throat.

After a frozen moment, he jerked into movement and handed over a mug. 'You must think I'm crazy, forgetting Matt.'

'Well, your memory's not very good. You forgot to make his lunch too.'

He sat opposite Laura. 'I didn't forget that.'

'No.' She smiled. 'I know.'

He lost the ability to speak. All he could do was absorb the warmth of her smile. It seeped through him, thawing his blood.

'I'm sorry for encouraging him. He's so hard to resist.'

'You're telling me? I don't have a hope.'

'You've done a super job of raising him. He's a lovely little boy.'

'Thanks.' He looked down, swirling his coffee. She could have no idea how much it meant to hear her say that. 'Laura—'

'I brushed my teeth, Dad,' Matt said from the doorway. 'I'm ready for my story.'

Craig put the coffee mug on an end table and linked his hands to stop them shaking. 'Be there in a minute, mate.' He waited for Matt to run off to his bedroom, then looked at Laura. This could be his only chance to tell her how he felt. He had to take it.

'Laura, I've missed you more than you

can imagine. I know now that you were my one and only.'

Her eyes shone, wet. 'Were? Past tense?'

'Were. Are. Always will be. I'm so sorry I believed the worst when I heard you'd been seen with someone else. It was immature of me. You must hate me.'

Tears escaped from her eyes and slid down her cheeks. 'I don't hate you. I was hurt, yes, but I couldn't hate you. I loved you too much.'

His chest tightened till he could hardly breathe. He moved to sit next to her. His hands trembled as he reached out to cup her sweet, tear-streaked face.

'Loved? Past tense?'

'I still love you,' she whispered.

He felt as though he'd come round from a coma. Life pulsed through him as he held her against his heart. 'Be mine again, Laura,' he said as he brushed his lips against her temple.

'*Dad*!'

Matt's voice calling from the bedroom brought Craig back to his senses. He'd forgotten him for a second time. How could he expect Laura to want him when he already had a child? Another woman's son?

He released her. 'I'm sorry. Matt changes everything. It's not fair on you.'

'Don't say that,' she said quickly. 'I want us to be together, Craig.'

'But—'

Laura slipped her hands around his neck and touched her lips to his. 'I love Matt. I've had time to get to know him. I want to help you take care of him.'

He took her in his arms again and laid his cheek against the remembered softness of her hair. 'We have so much to talk about.'

'Yes,' she said gently, 'but first let's read a story to Matt. We have the rest of our lives to talk.'

'Just talk?'

Her eyes sparkled and, taking his hand, she tugged him to his feet.

He held on tightly to Laura's hand and led her from the room. He'd learned his lesson well. He'd never let her go again. ■

Horoscopes

Find out what 2008 holds for you! **By Dadhichi Toth**

AQUARIUS

21 January — 18 February

Romance and Friendship

Friendships are fun and alluring in 2008. Venus highlights your ability to make some exciting love contacts, especially if you've felt like a wallflower for some time.

In February you'll feel stimulated socially and emotionally but could be overly unrealistic in your expectations. Keep your feet firmly planted on planet Earth.

A thrilling romance lifts your spirits in April and this culminates in a permanent arrangement in July or August. For attached Aquarians it's a loving and intimate period for you.

You are ambitious with your partner between June and September but guard against quarrels. You want your own way and this will cause problems.

Sexual frustrations occur in August and September but are an opportunity for growth, not a problem! This will signal you to speak about your feelings more.

Profession and Finances

Work and finances pick up steam in February but will be deadlocked in March with the Sun causing monetary worries. Spend less to save more.

Your chance for a new position in July will be a welcome relief from drudgery in your profession. You'll be afraid to make the jump if a new job is offered though.

From September to December Mars, Venus and the Sun crown you with amazing successes. It's a successful cycle for you but don't let it go to your head.

Luck and Opportunities

Luck is stronger in the last quarter of the year and dazzlingly so if you work slowly and diligently in the first part of 2008. Expect a lift financially in the coming 12 months.

PISCES

19 February — 20 March

Romance and Friendship

Making a strong impression wherever you go will be an important component of your character in 2008. You realise that your personal style will be more noticeable and this will pay off romantically.

A stroke of social luck in February brings new friends with extra respect and favours thrown in for good measure. A new introduction will benefit you.

Family worries in March clear up by April but your sense of duty will over- shadow your partying or romanticising mood. In May you'll spend big to look your best for that new soul-mate on the scene.

Saturn's influence on your marriage can make you feel as if permanent love is delayed. Look at the positive side of relationships and don't scare away potential lovers with negativity.

In August and September, your wildest fantasies come true! Intimacy is strong and genuine feelings of love are reciprocated. This sets a sunny trend for the rest of the year.

Profession and Finances

You are unsettled professionally, especially till March. After this you are focused and ready for business.

You'll build up plenty of momentum for work projects but feel pretty overwhelmed and exhausted by August due to smothering circumstances. Prioritise and delegate.

Employers favour you after October and nominate you for bigger and brighter things. The catch? More responsibility unfortunately!

Luck and Opportunities

Your luck is in the form of good associations this year. Don't turn your back on new introductions which open doors for you especially in October.

ARIES

21 March — 20 April

Romance and Friendship

The coming year will fill you with charm as Mercury and the Sun usher in fresh social circumstances in February.

A relationship suffers because of your popularity but March is a great time to rebuild your love. Family is strong during April when Mars dominates.

In July and August your diary will be full so manage your time well. There's a strong cultural connection in September with your artistic talents shining.

Fortunately in October and November your sexual needs are fulfilled and you'll explore new fantasies with a loved one.

The Moon, Venus and Jupiter forecast continuing luck.

Profession and Finances

You have an endless supply of ambition this year. In January the high-powered Sun and Jupiter promise an active work schedule. Don't forget — slow and steady wins the race.

In February team efforts will build your success. Fiends are lucky for your employment in March but in April expenses may get out of hand.

By May you should have a clear plan about work and money. June and July are speculative months and I see you taking the stock market by storm.

In the last part of the year your health will be crucial to getting ahead. Dynamic partnerships and negotiations are on the cards in and after October.

Luck and Opportunities

You're lucky socially especially in March when your ideas will be received well. Mercury and Venus spark your influence over others.

Your lucky breaks are a gift from Jupiter, your luckiest planet. Aries, enjoy the year!

TAURUS

21 April — 21 May

Romance and Friendship

This will be an important year for your love life. Your aura will attract many people. After February, however, you'll cut free from an exhausting relationship.

In March Venus showers you with love. You'll feel completely new. During April you'll meet many remarkable people, forming fascinating friendships.

Demanding relatives want their pound of flesh during June and July so don't be too weak-willed in standing up for your rights.

Expect wild and wonderful times in August. The Sun, Mars and Uranus challenge your traditional safety net. In September surrender time to lend a hand to a loved one.

During October dazzling occasions for love come your way. Relationships deepen. Love interferes with personal ambitions in December so difficult choices are likely.

Profession and Finance

Success is strong in February when the Sun boosts your career. In March you'll save money and feel secure with your spending habits under control.

Risk taking is in full swing throughout April. The Sun in your zone of loss causes a devil-may-care attitude. A hard luck story in April will catch you off guard. In May, you can transfer to another job with a fatter pay cheque.

Your personal appeal is strong so put it to good use in May and June. Business partnerships with family members are lucky during October.

After November you'll generate new avenues of growth professionally. You'll expand your own business if you're independently employed.

Luck and Opportunities

Jupiter will spend the year in your region of luck. Expect handsome rewards without too much effort. March and April are significant for happiness, wealth and professional advancement.

GEMINI

22 May — 22 June

Romance and Friendship

Anticipate harmonious relationships in 2008. You will be popular as Venus works its magic on your romantic and social affairs.

Jupiter in your zone of sexuality creates stronger intimate connections, and romantic opportunities are plentiful between January and April.

Mercury dominates your romantic affairs throughout October. Unfinished emotional business will be resolved so that you can move on to better things and generally enjoy life in a more relaxed manner.

In November love planet Venus adds spice to your life, being in your marriage zone. If engagement or marriage is on your mind, speak about it.

In December harmonious relationships and a greater understanding of others is the likely outcome of your efforts.

Profession and Finance

'Nothing ventured, nothing gained' applies perfectly in the coming 12 months. The Sun activates your career in March and a greater sense of self-worth occurs.

During April, Mars and Jupiter lift your thinking to a new level. You will make far-reaching plans and take risks you ordinarily wouldn't.

Speculative investments in September are a good move if you're courageous enough. They'll be lucrative after the Sun enters your zone of speculation in October.

From October to December Jupiter creates an added bonus for your security. Financial gains will be very satisfying.

Luck and Opportunities

Through a stroke of luck, you'll be the beneficiary of others' hard work. Lap it up, Gemini-that's a great bonus for you so don't feel guilty about enjoying these fruits fully!

CANCER

23 June — 22 July

Romance and Friendship

You'll want more out of life in 2008. Unfortunately not everyone will understand your grand gestures and this will cause some rejection.

In March your popularity will be a hit with the Sun moving and shaking, rocking and rolling things socially. Your love affairs blossom after May.

Romances are at a fork in the road of life in October when your ideals are mismatched with the reality of a situation. Take off your rose-coloured glasses.

In the last week of November your health will wane and you'll prefer to stay out of the limelight for a while.

Expect a great conclusion to the year when Venus joins hands with Jupiter. Love is the cherry on top of the cake in December.

Profession and Finances

In March you will achieve something special professionally. Don't be afraid to investigate alternative avenues of employment.

Look sharp and be prepared for intense meetings in May. Money is high on your agenda but then again disagreements surrounding the almighty buck could dampen your success. Be well informed with all the facts at your fingertips.

Pluto has an important part to play in your business partnerships in 2008. In November and December educate yourself and improve your skills.

Luck and Opportunities

If you've had a long-term health issue this is an excellent year when powerful curative energies flow your way. Look forward to a healing!

The months of February, March, April and September are superb. Expect Lady Luck to dazzle you. Love and money are coming your way.

LEO

23 July — 23 August

Romance and Friendship

The coming year brings remarkable changes in your personal life. Early on in the year focus on your partner. This will lift your relationship to new heights.

During April and May be more assertive but don't push others out of their comfort zone. In May mend rifts and ensure your family is mutually supportive. Eliminate long-standing grudges if you can.

You might be blessed with a child in 2008. Newlyweds or those seeking children will be lucky in this respect this year.

You'll have oodles of sex appeal in October but it mightn't be easy to act upon. Other things will tug at your heartstrings.

Don't overlook your intuition. Betrayal of trust could become a problem. When you seek out new friendships pay attention to character flaws.

Profession and Finances

You'll be a tireless worker and interested in organising your work and finances with razor-sharp precision.

Saturn creates a tendency to inflict perfection on others. Aspiring to better standards is useful but avoid being tyrannical.

By March you'll feel comfortable rejoining the 'team' and collaborating on new projects in which you'll play a leading role.

Ambitions swell in May and into July you'll hunt down anything that will help you achieve financial success.

Expect a fine finish to the year. Office modifications will result in a topsy-turvy state for a while.

Luck and Opportunities

Your luck in 2008 hinges on your ability to persuade others to help you. Jupiter's position shows that your positive and magnanimous energy is advantageous to you professionally.

VIRGO

24 August — 22 September

Romance and Friendship

Your social life will grow and expand during 2008. This will have to do with your push to assert your unique personality.

In March and June there's an upswing in romantic escapades and these will be ideal months to explore unusual avenues to find happiness.

In September, your daily routine and responsibilities may be thrown into some turmoil. You'll be challenged to sacrifice some of your precious time for relatives and other close loved ones.

You have the possibility of either pursuing committed relationships or equally playing the field and exploring what's on tap in a carefree, non-committed manner.

Your popularity will increase throughout October and November. You'll have a dynamic drive and your emotions will be passionate, even red hot.

Profession and Finances

You'll be vivacious and confident with money, expressing ingenuity through good connections and capitalising on them.

You have long-term ambitions you wish to bring to fruition. These desires will be fulfilled as you'll be disciplined.

In July and August you'll feel frustrated by employers. In September a revival occurs so don't worry.

In November and December, don't mix your professional or financial interests. Don't let work encroach on personal relationships either.

Be wary of deceptive characters who'll try to take advantage of you.

Luck and Opportunities

This will be a year in which you combine your serious desire for goal achievement and luck. Your belief systems will play a major role in achieving these goals.

Younger people will also somehow bring you luck. This has to be one of the best years on record.

LIBRA

23 September — 23 October

Romance and Friendship

You're crazy about love in 2008 and it's still going to be loads of fun. Dropping tradition in favour of outrageous romance is forecast.

Your passion prompts you to indulge yourself in April. You won't hang around waiting for others to pick up their pace. You'll explore new emotional territories to gain happiness.

During June your relationships will be unstable and will cloud your judgement. Mars spotlights friendships so make an extra effort to improve relationships at this time.

August reinvigorates your love life and till November continues to provide you with some balance. Sharing and appreciating beautiful things with the ones you love is assured.

Jupiter promotes romantic affairs and Neptune prompts you to believe in true love at last.

Profession and Finances

You're inclined to entrepreneurial activities and great successes arrive in April. You'll be ambitious throughout the coming twelve months but don't be cold-blooded in pursuing your goals.

In May and June your income will increase. A restructuring of your finances is seen after July.

Your desire for success is strong in September and October with some fine opportunities to cash in on your efforts. A secondary source of income is forecast at this time

The dynamic influence of Mars on your professional life will cause you to surge ahead and feel a sense of real accomplishment.

Luck and Opportunities

Uranus treks through your work zone so luck is likely to improve through progressive thinking and novel work practices. In April, Mercury and Uranus assist your professional dreams to materialise. Good luck Libra!

SCORPIO

24 October — 22 November

Romance and Friendship

This will be an emotionally fulfilling year. You'll approach life with a positive attitude. Mercury, the Sun and Jupiter sharpen your communication. Your words will win hearts.

You will gain powerful insights into the true motivations of yourself and others and will weed out insincere friends early in the year.

Activities involving clubs, societies and study groups will bring you romantic opportunities but in July you will feel frustrated with loved ones and will be misunderstood.

August is busy socially and an element of surprise through unexpected meetings will take your breath away.

In September your love affairs are exciting but also challenging. If you're single you'll take rash measures which might eventually embarrass you.

In October you'll feel washed out but that will pass in November when Cupid revisits you.

The coming year will be an exciting time when you open up to new emotional possibilities.

Profession and Finances

Saturn in your social sphere means past contacts start to bear fruit. Doors will open through your association with important people.

Some Scorpios will find themselves catapulted from average financial circumstances to incredible affluence. February will be a time of hard work but if you've overspent, this will be more challenging.

The Sun and Saturn tweak your sense of duty in September. Spreading yourself too thin will impact on your performance and personal relationships.

Negotiations will, however, generally go smoothly in 2008.

Luck and Opportunities

Get in touch with your inner self this year. This secret of achieving more is by removing your negative traits. This is a sure-fire way to augment your success, luck and good karma.

SAGITTARIUS

23 November — 21 December

Romance and Friendship

The next year will be a period of extraordinary change. A new chapter in your emotional life unfolds. March brings unexpected lovers into your life. Jupiter and Uranus nudge you and you'll want plenty of friends surrounding you.

Sexual matters are going to take centre stage during July so expect lots of physical enjoyment.

Disagreements over lifestyle in August are bothersome. Open and sympathetic discussions are absolutely essential to resolve matters.

Passion is again powerful in September with the union of Mars, Mercury and Venus.

Venus pulls back on its love vibes in October and this is your romantic lull in 2008. Deal with elements of your past relationships fairly and squarely.

A year that will be very satisfying emotionally.

Profession and Finances

Set up a foundation for success in January and February as your thinking is big in 2008. But don't get carried away by smooth talkers.

August and September are key months for your work. Profits will be high due to your first-class efforts.

Devote some time to co-workers. Too much work will pull you away from them and make you feel as though you're an island unto yourself.

Revitalising your physical health is essential. Your energy runs low in November due to the power planets Mars and Sun getting quieter.

Luck and Opportunities

Much of your luck is focused around money and material resources during 2008. The Sun and Jupiter combine in your finance zone, so it's a lucky year with greater prosperity.

In April, June, August and October Lady Luck, the Sun's messenger, offers astounding success.

CAPRICORN

22 December — 20 January

Romance and Friendship

In 2008 your confidence and positive radiance will be at an all-time high. The world is your oyster.

In February Venus brings your family into harmony. Your domestic scene will be fulfilling. In April expect family reunions. Beautify your home and take pride in your family.

For singles, July is a time to take your relationship to the marriage stage. Throughout August your sexual needs come to the forefront. You'll remove negative feelings and past experiences that encroach on your relationships.

October brings a well-earned break with a loved one. Recharge your batteries together. After November Venus revisits your Sun sign bringing back that buzz into your life. Love and beauty will peak.

Profession and Finances

You want excitement and will do away with anything routine this year. Mars and Uranus prompt economic independence.

Throughout February and March financial planning will be uppermost in your mind as you reorient your material goals. Consult a good financial planner.

Stimulating yet demanding business activities keep you on the edge of your seat between May and June but you'll improve your efficiency at work and with money.

New partnerships are made in July and greater teamwork in November decompresses your working life.

Luck and Opportunities

In September and October the Sun brings luck your way with the chance of some award or gift being presented to you. This will make you feel appreciative and grateful for the life you have. You deserve whatever you achieve in 2008.

For more visit
www.astrology.com.au

Pure reading pleasure.

Available from WHSmith, ASDA, Tesco and a...

Puzzle Solutions

Show Words — Page 148

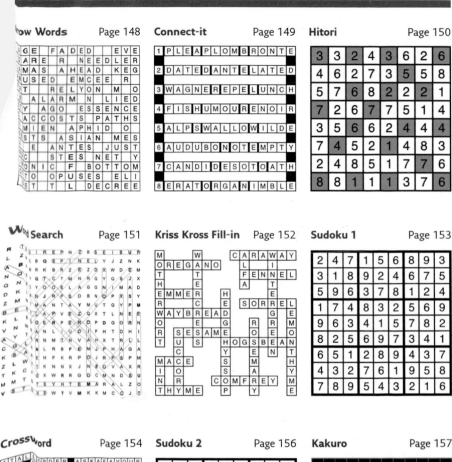

Connect-it — Page 149

1	P	L	E	A	P	L	O	M	B	R	O	N	T	E
2	D	A	T	E	D	A	N	T	E	L	A	T	E	D
3	W	A	G	N	E	R	E	P	E	L	U	N	C	H
4	F	I	S	H	U	M	O	U	R	E	N	O	I	R
5	A	L	P	S	W	A	L	L	O	W	I	L	D	E
6	A	U	D	U	B	O	N	O	T	E	M	P	T	Y
7	C	A	N	D	I	D	E	S	O	T	O	A	T	H
8	E	R	A	T	O	R	G	A	N	I	M	B	L	E

Hitori — Page 150

3	3	2	4	3	6	2	6
4	6	2	7	3	5	5	8
5	7	6	8	2	2	2	1
7	2	6	7	7	5	1	4
3	5	6	6	2	4	4	4
7	4	5	2	1	4	8	3
2	4	8	5	1	7	7	6
8	8	1	1	1	3	7	6

Word Search — Page 151

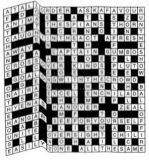

Kriss Kross Fill-in — Page 152

Sudoku 1 — Page 153

2	4	7	1	5	6	8	9	3
3	1	8	9	2	4	6	7	5
5	9	6	3	7	8	1	2	4
1	7	4	8	3	2	5	6	9
9	6	3	4	1	5	7	8	2
8	2	5	6	9	7	3	4	1
6	5	1	2	8	9	4	3	7
4	3	2	7	6	1	9	5	8
7	8	9	5	4	3	2	1	6

Crossword — Page 154

Sudoku 2 — Page 156

5	7	2	9	8	3	4	1	6
4	8	3	2	6	1	9	5	7
6	9	1	4	7	5	2	8	3
8	6	4	3	2	9	1	7	5
2	1	9	7	5	6	8	3	4
7	3	5	8	1	4	6	9	2
3	5	6	1	9	2	7	4	8
1	2	7	5	4	8	3	6	9
9	4	8	6	3	7	5	2	1

Kakuro — Page 157